NICKEL PACKAGE

Books by David Chill

Post Pattern

Fade Route

Bubble Screen

Safety Valve

Corner Blitz

Nickel Package

Double Pass

NICKEL PACKAGE

A Novel By

DAVID CHILL

Cover art photography provided by Matthew Chill

For Greg Martin

One

It was supposed to have been a routine background investigation. Just gather some information on a high-profile job candidate. No one was supposed to die.

"We're looking for a new CEO," declared the wily executive. "Chief Executive Officer."

"Too bad for me," I said with a wink. "I just signed a 12-month lease for office space."

The wily executive smiled patiently, but it was not a genuine smile. He wore a white shirt and a green tie, and I was certain that both were very expensive. His name was Nick Roche, and his handsome office provided a view that reached the glistening Pacific. It had rained this past weekend, our first storm in over a month, and the air was now sun-washed and pristine. From my seat on his soft leather couch, I could almost see Catalina Island.

"Jay told me you had a wise-guy streak in you," he said.

"Glad you've been put on notice. You know, they used to refer to CEOs as Presidents. I gather that's *passé now*."

"Very much so. Especially here at BMB. We have a lot of Presidents. I'm President of Operations."

I tried to look impressed. Big egos need reinforcement, especially in this town. There is a highly visceral need to show off, whether it's in or out of the office. In the boardroom or on the streets. It's not unusual to be driving along in L.A. and be surrounded on all sides by Porsches and Mercedes. Or by the occasional Rolls-Royce.

"Mr. Burnside," he continued, "my brother-in-law also told me you're very astute."

"As is Jay," I smiled. Anyone who calls me astute deserves to be repaid in kind.

Roche shrugged. "He makes decent money, anyhow."

I continued to smile, although the last comment gave me pause. For the past three years, I had taken a career detour, a move that had earned me a boatload of money. Gobs of money. More money than a P.I. like me could ever make, and ridiculously more than the salary I once earned as an LAPD officer. But what Jay and I had earned was likely a pittance when compared with Nick Roche's income.

"Money isn't everything," I said, hoping he wouldn't counter by telling me that, no, in fact, money was the only thing. Thankfully, he did not.

The past few years had been lucrative for me, but the process had taken its toll. The hundred-hour work weeks were the proof. And even if USC's new head coach had asked me to stay on as a well-heeled assistant, I wouldn't have done so. I had even rejected the opportunity to join my old friend Johnny Cleary in the NFL. My son was now three years old, and I had missed so much. I didn't hear him say his first words, and I didn't see him take his first steps. There were some things money could not buy, and some jobs that were not worth the personal price. I needed to make a course correction.

"Look," Roche said, directing the conversation back to the matter at hand. "We need help here from someone who's smart. And discreet. And thorough."

"All right. So tell me. Just who are these CEO candidates?"

Roche pulled a pack of cigarettes from his drawer, slid one out and lit it. I thought of reminding him that smoking, even inside private office buildings, was illegal in California. I also thought of my fee going up in smoke, and decided to be really astute and exercise some restraint.

"We have a number of people," he said, blowing a plume of smoke up at the ceiling. "But there's one in particular who excites the board. His name is Eric Starr. You might have heard the name."

I shook my head. "Sorry. Unless he's good at covering wide receivers, I probably wouldn't have paid much attention. At least not for the past three years."

"I understand," he said. "Jay's told me the hours you guys put in. I guess coaching is a full-time job and then some. He also filled me in on your background. Quite a career you've had. College football star, LAPD officer, private detective, coaching football at USC. You've certainly had a marvelous life."

"It's far from over," I pointed out. "I'm just shifting gears."

"Sorry," he said. "No offense intended."

"None taken. So tell me about this Eric Starr," I said.

"I'll give you the topline," Roche said. "Grew up in Orange County, father's a high level executive with a tech firm. Eric spent a couple of years working there, then he and a colleague got this idea for a startup. The two of them went out on their own, they began the Laputa Company. You've heard of that, haven't you?"

"Sure. Everyone has."

"Right. A few years later, Laputa's grown into this big Internet giant. It's got everything. It's a media outlet that provides news and content. It's a search engine, an ISP, a social media site and an online retailer. Eric didn't create the technology, but he grabbed the reins and made it a success. He's more of a marketing guy."

"And he's willing to give up his baby to come work for BMB?"

"It's complicated. We're in discussions. BMB's twenty times bigger than Laputa, and he'd oversee a movie studio, TV networks, theme parks and video games. We're a huge business. This could be a good next step for him."

"So he'd be your boss."

"I've got a contract. I'm not concerned about my future."

"Okay. And you think Eric's the guy to run BMB."

Roche shrugged and held up his palms. "Some people on the board think so. He's got a track record of success. And he can bring fresh thinking to a 75 year-old company."

"But there are concerns about Eric," I remarked.

"There are."

"Tell me about them."

Roche leaned back in his sleek black leather chair and stopped the dialogue. He appeared as if he were deep in thought, reviewing what he knew and maybe pondering what nuggets should be revealed to me. He reached down and fingered the end of his green tie. Then, taking a long drag on his cigarette, he let the smoke slowly waft out through his nostrils.

"Eric has a history," he began, an air of drama filling the room along with the smoke. "He makes quick decisions. He's often right, mind you, but he flies by the seat of his pants. In the tech world, you can get away with that, everything moves so quickly you can recover from your mistakes. Over here, a decision to greenlight a movie or build a new theme park means investing hundreds of millions of dollars. Being wrong can have severe consequences."

"Sounds like you've studied Laputa."

"A bit. A couple of our former execs moved over there. They talk."

"Okay, fine," I said. "But I know as much about corporate life as you do about football schemes. Just what are you really after?"

Roche took a glance out the window, his deep pondering starting to morph into a look of annoyance. My comments frequently had that effect on people. But it also spurred them to talk, often more so than they intended. Occasionally, a gem of information would materialize.

"Eric's personal life is an issue as well. Big partier, bad

behavior with women, not using good judgment. You name it."

I raised my eyebrows. "Well, that never happens in show biz, does it?"

"You have to understand," he said, his voice now displaying his impatience, "we've gone through three CEOs in the past four years. We're a publicly traded company. Fortune 500. This isn't just about hiring another yahoo in to run a movie studio. We need a visionary. Someone who can lead us into the future."

"Okay. I can dig into his background. But let me ask you something. Three CEOs in four years? This job sounds like a revolving door. Why is that?"

"A few reasons," he said. "Mostly, they didn't deliver results. Some bad decisions. These days, a CEO is judged every quarter on financial results. A few bad quarters and they're out. It can be as simple as a number of flops at the box office. Our most recent CEO, Malcolm Taylor, he was only here for a year before he resigned. There were some personal issues. But he wasn't cutting it either."

"Sounds like it's easy to fail here."

"It's easy to fail everywhere, Mr. Burnside. And all of the past CEOs came up through the ranks at BMB. Our core business is the movie studio and that's where these guys made their bones. Production execs. Entertainment types. But it hasn't worked out, so the board's looking for something different. Can't keep doing the same thing and expect different results. You know. Sisyphus rolling the rock uphill and all that."

"Why don't they bump up someone like you?"

He smiled again. "Our company's roots are still in show biz. I have an MBA. From Harvard. But people look at me as a suit. The board doesn't think suits have the creative vision. I'm not complaining, mind you. I'm paid extremely well for what I do. But moving up isn't going to be an option for someone like me."

"All right. You mentioned a few internal candidates. You want me to look into them, too?"

"No. I think we have enough on our internal people. But it's unusual that outsiders are even considered. This is new terrain for us. So we want you to look into Eric's background, garner any insights you can."

"What about my talking to Eric himself?" I asked.

"No," he shook his head definitively. "The board doesn't want any footprints."

"That's going to be difficult," I pointed out. "When you start talking with friends and colleagues, word spreads. It can't help but get back to that person."

"Jay said you were good. You'll figure it out."

I paused for a moment and considered this. Then I tried to think about something else. I looked around his office. The walls held real artwork, cheerful splotches of color that probably meant something to the artist. The splotches meant little to me, other than they were pretty to look at and most likely cost the buyer a ton of money.

"So tell me more about this board you've been referring to," I said.

"Board of directors. It's made up of CEOs from other companies, a few politicians, dignitaries, couple of academics. They provide oversight. There's even a USC professor on our board, Dr. Lucas Kanter, maybe you recall him. He teaches at the film school there. Cinematic arts."

"Don't know the man, I didn't mingle much with professors. But I'm surprised you didn't pick someone from the Marshall School. USC's business program is one of the best in the country."

"The board is largely selected by the CEOs," he shrugged. "They bring in people they know and trust. Occasionally they appoint their friends. Some CEO from Disney once added the principal from his son's grade school to his board. Then he added an actor."

"And they both got approved?"

"CEOs are given a lot of leeway on things. They have enormous power. That's why we're being especially careful. Our stock price has been getting hammered. Shareholders want to see results. And fast. As I said, we can't afford any more mistakes."

I thought about something. "Do you have a Security Director here?"

"Of course."

"What's his involvement been?"

"Well, Ferris looked into Eric initially. But we need an outsider now. That's where you come in."

"Ferris. Is that Hector Ferris?"

"Yes, he reports up to me. You know him?"

"Worked briefly with him at the Broadway Division of LAPD. Long time ago. Hector made Lieutenant, if I recall."

"That's right. He joined us a couple of years back.

Right after he retired from the police department. Thorough guy."

I agreed. Hector Ferris was certainly thorough, maybe too much so. I didn't tell Roche that Ferris's retirement was orchestrated by the chief, who got tired of him poking his self-righteous nose into every nook and cranny. The chief of police is like any other executive. Appreciative of hard work, but more than willing to cut the cord on someone who gets under their skin.

"Can I speak with Hector?"

Roche hesitated. "I suppose," he said, thinking about it for a minute. "Sure. I'll take you down to his office."

"So then I'll start today," I said.

"Good."

"You're aware of what my rate is," I said, a bit apprehensively. Normally it was a thousand dollars a day, although that was three years ago. And BMB was my first paying client since hanging out my shingle again. Given the plush corporate surroundings though, as well as my newfound high-income expectations, I needed to brand myself as a top-notch investigator. Charging a high fee was an effective way to create the impression you were good. So my special rate for BMB would be fifteen hundred a day. Plus expenses.

"I am indeed aware," Roche agreed, getting to his feet. "And Jay tells me you have a son who's preschool age. This should help cover part of the cost."

"I guess Jay's been pretty chatty. I'll have to chide him about using some discretion. In fact, I'm having lunch with him later."

Roche smiled. "Southern barbecue is Jay's favorite. Comfort food for him."

"I'm expanding his horizons. We're going old-school L.A. He'll like it. But tell me. How urgent is this background check?"

"It's for the board, so everything is urgent. Corporate life, you know. I'll assume this should only take a few days. This is Monday. I'd like something by the end of the week."

"Fine," I said. "I normally get an upfront fee. Couple of days to cover expenses."

Roche gave me a condescending look. "This is a multinational corporation. I don't keep a petty cash drawer," he said. "Send me an invoice."

*

The office Hector Ferris occupied was nowhere near as plush as Nick Roche's, nor did it have much of a view. There was a window, but it faced a parking lot. There were pictures hanging on the walls, but these were prints of classic movie posters, not original artwork. Hector sat in a black leather chair, but it was not as showy and there was no couch nearby. The two seats facing the desk were standard-issue gray cloth, and were utilitarian to boot. In one, however, sat an attractive woman.

"Hector," Roche announced, bouncing inside and motioning me to follow. "This is the fellow I was telling you about. Mr. Burnside has heard of you."

"And I've heard of him, too," he said, rising and

shaking my hand lightly. "Mister Private Eye."

"Lieutenant."

"It's no longer Lieutenant," he said. "You can call me Mr. Ferris."

"Sure, Hector. Whatever you say."

Ferris paused. "I remember you now from Broadway Division. You were a good cop. Then you turned into a smartass."

"I always was. I just hid it well."

The attractive woman stood up and extended her hand. She had tawny eyes and a wide-cut mouth, pretty, but in an L.A. sort of way. Slender, mildly buxom, and her face reflected a well-honed use of cosmetics. She looked good while appearing not to try. She had well-behaved, straight auburn hair that stopped right at her shoulders. From her ears dangled a pair of small, sparkling diamonds.

"Patty Muckenthaler," she announced. "President of Production."

I shook her hand. "You have a firm grip," I said, not telling her that it was stronger and less moist than Hector's.

"Why, thank you. I'm flattered," she said, overtly batting her eyelashes a few times.

"Patty," Roche nodded at her, "I hope everything's all right. Didn't think I'd see you in the Security Director's office today. Someone hitting on you again?"

"Nothing Hector and I can't handle," she smiled confidently. "Don't worry, Nick. It won't cost you any money. I know how you worry about the bottom line."

"Someone around here has to," Roche commented.

"Well, my business here is finished for now," she said and casually handed me her card. "Private eye, huh? I'll bet you have a lot of good stories."

"More than I can tell."

Patty Muckenthaler gave me a final smile and a wink as she walked out. "If you'd ever like to share, I just might want to hear about a few."

Roche looked back at Ferris as the pretty woman walked out into the hallway. "I'll leave you two to talk shop," he said and hurried out the door to catch up with Patty.

Ferris pointed to a chair as he moved behind his desk, easing himself gingerly down into his seat. He was a portly man with a wide girth and black, curly hair. He wore a navy jacket over a cheap yellow shirt with a clip-on tie, and looked every bit like the classic ex-cop with an office job. Ferris maintained a placid expression, but there were lines of age cutting across his forehead, and jowls were forming under his wide jaw. The only thing that struck me as out of place was the lump under his left armpit. That meant he was prepared for adverse situations. As was I.

"Burnside," he studied me. "Didn't know you very well when you were on the job."

"I knew you, though."

Ferris made a small choking sound and said nothing.

"Sounds like you heard some stories about me," I said.

"Sure. Who didn't? Officer Burnside. You were famous. And not in a good way. How did you wind up here on the BMB lot?"

"Friends in high places," I smiled.

"And you're investigating our future CEO."

"That's my assignment. Anything you want to tell?"

Ferris gave me a long stare. I looked him in the eye for a few moments, got bored, and turned toward his window. Not much was happening in the parking lot, either.

"Yeah, there's something I want to tell you," Ferris said, and I turned back to him. "This investigation on Eric Starr? It's mine. I started it and I want to finish it. You need to report to me. Whatever you learn, I want to know about it."

"That's nice. Makes sense, too. But, no, sorry."

"No?" he asked, eyebrows arching.

"No. I was hired by Nick Roche. I'm being paid out of Nick Roche's budget. He approves my invoices. I report to him, not you."

"You don't make friends easily, do you?"

"Neither do you, if I recall. Look, Hector," I sighed, "I want to work with you. Not against you. But my rules are pretty straightforward. They're not negotiable. When I find out something, you'll be the second call I make."

Ferris gazed at me some more. Then, as if some magical wand of acceptance had been waved over him, a sense perhaps, that arguing with me would be fruitless, he reached into his desk and came out with a manila file. He put on a pair of gold-framed reading glasses and perused some papers. "Eric Starr. Quite a success story. He built a great fortune over at Laputa."

"As they say, behind every great fortune is a great crime."

Ferris looked up at me again, still maintaining his placid expression. I wasn't even sure he had heard me. "Eric does have some history," he finally said, "but nothing that would prevent him from taking the reins here."

"Tell me about his history."

"You know about his partner and the accident?"

"Partner?"

"Business partner," he said, frowning. "It was all over the news. Jack Beale. Couple of years ago. Took his boat out one day with some friends, did a booze cruise. Everyone having a good time, just sailing along on the ocean blue. Then someone noticed Jack wasn't there. Not on the boat, nowhere."

"Only one exit," I said.

"Yeah, and the ocean's an awfully big place to search. His body never washed ashore. Probably wound up somewhere in the middle of the Pacific."

"Think he was pushed?"

"Always a possibility. Best anyone could figure is he got drunk and somehow fell in. But there were about ten people on the boat and their stories all matched. It was finally ruled an accident. Can't have a homicide without a body. Or a murder weapon. Or a witness."

"Was Eric on the boat?"

"Nope, he was actually in New York at the time. Can't beat that for an alibi. I guess the epilogue is what happened to the company. The terms of their partner agreement. If one partner wasn't around, the other would assume control. Eric became king of the hill. Jack's wife got nothing. When someone disappears, they have to wait seven years before the missing person's declared dead."

"You've done your homework. Anything else?"

"Nothing out of the ordinary. I mean, if we were hiring a traditional CEO, Eric would be taken out of the consideration pool right away. But not around here. There's been some behavioral issues. Drugs, a few fights. You sometimes see this in guys who launch Internet startups. Not a lot of boundaries."

"As opposed to the entertainment industry," I observed.

"There are similarities, sure."

"Think there's more?"

"I know there's more," he said, somewhat earnestly. "I just can't pry the details out of anybody. Everyone knows I'm with BMB and they won't speak with me. That's why you're here."

"Any suggestions where I should start?"

"How about at the beginning?"

I rolled my eyes. Everyone is just so witty these days. "All right," I said. "I'll poke around. Who've you talked to so far?"

"Mostly colleagues at Laputa. They all say he's brilliant. A little crazy. But they won't go into details."

"A little crazy isn't bad sometimes," I mused. "Can lead you to new things. Ideas you never thought of."

"Right. Maybe you should head up our search committee. I'll go ask the chairman of the board to step aside."

"Maybe you should. Say, let me ask you about that

Patty."

Ferris raised his eyebrows. "What about her?"

"Roche made a comment about someone hitting on her. Anything to that?"

"What do you care?"

I shrugged. "Just curious. That's why I like P.I. work. Might mean nothing, might mean something."

Ferris looked at me curiously. "Sorry. There are some things I don't talk about."

"Well now you've got my attention."

"Look, there's nothing to most of this sexual harassment stuff," Ferris said dismissively. "Half of it is meaningless banter. For some guys, a sleazy remark is just their way of flirting. Once in a while, there really is harassment, but proving it is another story. He said, she said. I talk to the people involved, tell them about company policy, give them lessons in manners. It usually doesn't amount to much. Once in a while it does."

"Patty's cute. And flirtatious. I'm sure she draws a lot of attention. And some stray comments, too."

"I'm sure it's happened," he said, his voice sounding both annoyed and strained. "But did you stop and think about the possibility that maybe Patty wasn't the one being harassed here?"

I sat back in my gray cloth chair. No, I hadn't thought about that.

Two

It was a pleasant day in late March. Most days in Los Angeles were pleasant. I had called Johnny Cleary last week, and he was still shoveling snow off his driveway in suburban Chicago. In places like the Upper Midwest, spring is a cruel joke that lasts a few weeks, sandwiched between a bitter-cold winter and a sweltering summer. In L.A. however, spring extends for most of the year. Los Angeles is one of the warmest places in the winter and one of the coolest in the summer. Hardly fair, but the temperate climate comes with a toxic stew of smog, rage-inducing traffic jams, and the constant threat of an earthquake that could level the entire region. It is a balance which many of us endure for the enjoyment of nice weather.

I walked into the Apple Pan, and its horseshoe shaped counter was almost full. The Apple Pan has been around since World War II and is now a classic L.A. icon. They serve burgers, a few sandwiches, pie, and not much more. The drinks are delivered in old-fashioned paper cones inserted into red plastic cup-holders. The waiters move at a frenetic pace and dress in the same starched white shirts and white garrison caps as when I had first visited, many years ago.

Near a corner sat a very large man working a very small phone. A copy of Sports Illustrated was strategically placed on the chair next to him, signaling the seat was reserved. He wore tan khakis and a bright blue golf shirt with the letters U-C-L-A written in script over the left pocket. This declaration of newfound loyalty came off as somewhat unnatural, and it frankly didn't look good on him.

"Jay Strong," I said, handing him the Sports Illustrated. "Nice to see you again. I almost didn't recognize you in your new disguise."

"Coach B!" he barked in his deep, gravelly voice, standing up and giving me a bear hug. I hugged him back, albeit more in self-defense. "You're looking well for an unemployed man."

"Self-employed," I corrected him, as we sat down. "Big difference."

"Call it what you will. I can't even imagine not being part of a football team. It's in my blood."

"You bleed powder blue now. Bruin colors. I can't imagine what *that's* like."

Jay Strong laughed a hearty laugh. The waiter came by quickly and we ordered: a tuna sandwich for me; two hickory burgers, fries and a can of Diet Coke for him.

"Gotta keep my strength up," he said. "Spring practice and all."

"How's it going over there in Westwood?"

Jay shrugged. To him, this was just another gig. Assistant coaches gravitated from school to school, often staying only a couple of years at any one place. It was part of the life. For some, it was a means to an end, a path to climb up a rung in the coaching ladder or advance into a more prestigious program. For Coach Jay, this job had the appearance of a lateral move. If that.

"Not what I planned on," he said.

"I just can't imagine someone switching from USC to UCLA. It's like switching blue or gray uniforms in the Civil War. You're either a Trojan or a Bruin. On one side or the other."

Jay shook his head. "Coaches. We're all just hired guns. Soldiers of fortune. I liken it to working in the business world. People can move from working at Coke to working at Pepsi. Or from Ford to Nissan. You go where you're appreciated. Ken Norton Jr. played for UCLA and then couldn't get hired there after his NFL career ended. So he came over and coached at USC. Kennedy Pola went the other route."

"So tell me. What's it like? Can't be the same as working for Johnny."

"It's not the same," he admitted. "Different coaching styles. Johnny gave us a lot more autonomy with the players. Plus, Johnny was better at the other stuff, dealing with kids' parents and the like. You get these helicopter dads who demand to know why their kid isn't getting playing time. At SC, you'd just send them straight to the head coach. Johnny would lay out exactly why, and then he'd tell them what their kid needs to do to get on the field. Over here, they're leaving it more to the assistants to deal with. It's tricky."

"Touchy-feely stuff was never your thing, huh?"

"No," Jay sighed. "I'm a results guy. I get players ready to play. Dealing with prima donnas or their demanding dads isn't one of my strengths. And I've got one now that's a thorn in my side. Some rapper's kid. The player was iffy on even getting a football scholarship, but he got one, probably because his dad's a celeb. This is L.A. after all. But the kid doesn't take weight training seriously, and he's not going to see the field. Explaining all this to a dad who's been in some gunfights is a challenge. We've had a few tense moments."

"Didn't realize how tough Westwood is. And they say USC is the school in the bad neighborhood," I joked.

"Nothing is quite like it appears," he said, in a way that was almost wistful.

"Indeed," I said. I thought back to my decision to accept Johnny's offer to coach defensive backs at USC, which led me into the most challenging job I had ever undertaken. Johnny's teams had been enormously successful, so the school gave him latitude on hiring decisions. I had played college football for the Trojans many years ago but had no experience as a coach, so my learning curve was steep. As I discovered, though, I was good at it. I liked working with young athletes on the field, but I took the most pride in using football to prepare them for the real world.

All of my players were extraordinary athletes who knew the fundamentals of how to play cornerback and safety. I taught them the intangibles, the little pointers that would give them an edge in a high-profile game. But I also emphasized that winning can be applied to all aspects of life. And I made sure they were keenly aware that most college players don't go on to make millions in pro football. The NFL is hyper-competitive, and it can take just one injury to end an athletic career. The kids needed a road map for going forward if their dreams of a pro career never materialized. From my own painful experience, I could certainly attest to how the random wind of fate could alter anyone's plans.

"You know," Jay said, "I wanted to move out of L.A., but I've got some personal commitments that are keeping me in town."

"The spousal unit?" I asked.

"Uh-huh. My wife wanted us to stay in L.A. No, make that *demanded* we stay in L.A. I had some schools talking about bringing me on, maybe giving me a bump up. Washington State interviewed me for offensive coordinator. Next step after that would be head coach. But Kitty's job is here. So here I stay."

"Not a lot of filmmaking being done up in the Palouse," I observed. The Washington State campus was located on the Idaho border, a pretty section of the country, but also very isolated. Not good for someone wanting a career in the entertainment industry.

"This is where Kitty's opportunity is. When she first heard USC wanted me a few years ago, she couldn't get us on a plane to L.A. fast enough. She's what they call an executive in charge of production. Whatever that means."

"Sounds like it might be interesting work."

"Yeah, she likes it. These days we make tradeoffs when we're married. I'm sure you know about that. If you were single, you'd probably be coaching DBs for the Chicago Bears right now."

Maybe yes, maybe no. When Johnny took the head

coaching job for the Bears, he asked a few of his assistants to come along with him. I was one. Jay was not. The Bears flew Gail and I out to Chicago for a few days. The money was great, so was the opportunity. That is, if I had wanted to move up in the coaching hierarchy. There was also a law firm there that showed interest in hiring Gail. But something wasn't quite right. Chicago seemed like a great city, very livable. Good schools, good restaurants, easy to get around. The people I met were all solid folk. The climate was cold, but that wasn't the issue. In the end, Chicago just didn't feel like home to us. And perhaps more importantly, staying in coaching would have meant continuing a lifestyle that would exhaust a workaholic. In the end, it was not an option for someone who truly wanted to spend more time with his family.

"Can't really say," I shrugged. "If I were single I might have tried the NFL. Just like I tried coaching in the first place. It was an opportunity Johnny gave me. I think I was good at it. But what I mostly liked was working with the kids and teaching them some life lessons. It felt satisfying."

Jay thought about this for a moment. "Probably for the best that you passed on the Bears job," he said wryly. "Your definition of success is different. For most of us, success comes down to winning or losing. Getting the team to perform on the field when they need to. The other stuff, the personal connections, that's just gravy."

"You're the one who should have gone to the NFL," I laughed. "You've got the businesslike approach. That's the league. It's a business."

Jay gave me a hard look. "I wasn't asked. I wasn't part of Johnny's inner circle, Mr. Bond."

"Mr. Bond?" I peered at him.

"Bond," he repeated. "James Bond. That's what some of the other coaches used to call you."

"They thought I was Johnny's spy?"

"What else could they think? You got your job through a friendship. A contact. You never came up through the ranks."

I took this in. Johnny said he could see potential in people. He thought he saw it in me. I wasn't so sure, but a salary offer that extended well into six figures was enough to get me to bite. And Gail liked the idea of more money streaming in. At least she did at first.

"It's true," I admitted. "I got the job simply because Johnny knew me. But the spy part? No. Believe it or not, I never told Johnny what the assistant coaches were saying. And he never asked me."

"All right."

I had the sense Jay didn't quite believe me, but I saw no need to argue the point. I was out of coaching now, and that was that. Our food arrived, and we dug in. My sandwich was just like I remembered it, a big hunk of lettuce stuffed between the tuna and the rye bread, and some black olives on the side. I mooched a few fries from Jay and they brought back memories of childhood. Some recollections were good, some were bittersweet. My mom used to take me to the Apple Pan for a treat when I was a kid; it was about all we could afford. Neither the food nor its ambience had changed much over the decades. I got the feeling some of the guys working the counter had been there for many decades, too.

"So I do need to thank you," I said between bites. "Your referral to Nick Roche landed me a paying gig. It actually pays quite well."

"Happy to help," he said, grabbing a handful of fries. "You get to meet Slick Nick yet?"

"That's how you refer to your brother-in-law?" I asked.

"Only when I'm in a nice mood," he said. "Aw, it's all good, I guess. We're just from different worlds."

I imagined they were. Jay Strong was a good old boy from Mississippi, big and brawny, the kind you'd want on your side if the going got rough. He coached offensive linemen, a position he knew very well. Jay had been an offensive tackle, making all-SEC for three years at Ole Miss, a long time ago. His down-home personality wasn't really a fit here in L.A., but he was a natural at any college football program, and so that's where he spent the bulk of his days, happily secluded.

"It's hard to picture you and Nick being related. A buttoned-up Ivy Leaguer and a backwoods guy from the Deep South."

"Funny," he said, finishing his first burger and picking up the second. "But we're not blood. We just have the same taste in good-looking women. Our wives are sisters. Kitty's sister moved out here a few years ago to be an actress. She landed a few small parts, but then she landed Nick. Role of a lifetime, being married to a wealthy guy who likes to throw his money around."

"I see."

"Yeah. My wife studied film in college, but she didn't have much opportunity back home. Kitty worked as a news director for a station in Memphis. Moving to L.A. meant having a lot of opportunity. With Nick at BMB, she got her foot in the door there. She's got one feature film wrapping now, has a few irons in the fire for later this year. Pretty soon she'll get a shot at directing her own movie. Dream come true. For her."

The acrid tinge in his voice was evident. His wife's thriving career meant his would get stifled for a while. It was sometimes the price you paid for a marriage. Tradeoffs indeed. One partner's career gets put on hold for a while so the other's can flourish. But in the case of Jay and Kitty, I wasn't sure how this would play out over the long haul. The entertainment business had a huge presence in L.A. and New York, but not so much elsewhere. Options for this college football coach were going to be limited.

"Does your wife talk to you about BMB much?"

Jay shrugged. "Some. I used to think that watching over a bunch of college kids' high jinks was a challenge. According to Kitty, it's nothing compared to making a movie. I think one of the qualifications for being in that business is you have to be a flake. Or at least work hard at being one. And then there's the company politics. BMB is intense. You think coaches can be deceptive? These execs take that to a whole 'nother level."

"Different world from what she's used to?"

"Oh, yeah. She's navigating her way, but I don't think

she anticipated all of this."

"All of what?" I asked.

Jay finished the rest of his burger and signaled for another Diet Coke. "Ah, it's nothing," he said and tried to give me a wink. It was half-hearted, an attempt to try and reassure me that everything was under control.

"Anything Nick's involved in?"

Jay palmed the icy Diet Coke can carefully before cracking it open. "From what I understand, Nick's involved in a lot of things over there," he finally said.

A seat opened up and a young man in his early 20s sat down next to Jay and brushed against him slightly. Jay turned around and told him to watch what he was doing. The young man gave him a dirty look, and I thought he might make a smart crack. Then he took a good look at Jay's bulk, and perhaps more importantly, the hostility flaring from Jay's eyes, and thought better of it. He muttered an apology and picked up a menu. Jay turned back to me, but the remnants of that short, rancorous encounter remained on his face. I glanced up at the waiter and quickly made a can-we-get-the-check scribbling motion with my hand. A good way to end an awkward situation is to simply move away from it.

*

The LAPD's Purdue Division was located next to a courthouse, below Santa Monica Boulevard, and just a few blocks west of the San Diego Freeway. When I worked there, I used to frequent a coffee shop down the street that had terrific cinnamon rolls. That place, like too many others, was now just a fuzzy memory.

The surrounding area featured a series of nondescript three-story stucco apartment buildings, along with some modest single-family homes. That was before the real estate frenzy that began in the late 1990s. While affordable at one time, these houses now fetched close to a million dollars. Some people in L.A. were getting very rich, while others were tumbling through the cracks.

Captain Juan Saavedra was out in the field when I arrived, and his assistant didn't know when he'd be back. Always best to call first, she advised. I wandered around the station house for a few minutes, hoping to see a familiar face. Many years had passed since I had worn the badge, and those familiar faces were mostly gone. But I did see one, and when our eyes met, he waved me into his office. I also noticed the additional stripe he had attained.

"Sergeant De Santos," I grinned. "Congratulations on getting a bump up."

"Thanks," he said and motioned me to sit in a gray metal seat facing his desk. "Long time coming."

"If I recall correctly, you were thinking of moving on. You were hearing the siren call of becoming a P.I."

"Things change," he shrugged. "You know how it goes. Juan transferred back to Purdue last year, brought me over. Whenever I move with him, I get a promotion."

"Nice. Sounds like they don't want to you to leave. Not exactly a king's ransom, but a sergeant's pay isn't bad."

"Said the man who walked away from the golden goose."

"You heard."

"Yeah. I think you're nuts. Walking away from a lot of coin."

"You can't live your life just chasing money," I told him.

"When you got an ex-wife and child support? Oh, yes you can."

"I feel your pain."

"Probably not."

And I probably didn't. It is far easier to express sympathy for someone than to actually experience it in a prescient and meaningful way. I had met Roberto a few years ago when he was still down at the Broadway Division. Roberto was a second-generation Filipino immigrant, the type of officer the department had been seeking out for many years.

When I first joined the department, the LAPD was majority white. Today, the police demographics more closely reflect the diverse population of the city. The change was a part of the LAPD's attempt at community policing, the idea that greater sensitivity might be shown towards minorities if more people of color were on the job. In the end, I'm not sure how well this really worked. When a person puts on the badge and gun, their color transforms to the blue on their uniform. As a former chief of police liked to say, the LAPD was the toughest gang in town.

"So what brings you around these parts?" he asked.

"I have a new client. Just some background work. Figured I'd check with the guys who know the most."

"Who's your client?"

"BMB. Ring a bell?"

De Santos snorted. "Oh, yeah. Brings back a memory of my first week on the job. I was on traffic detail. Rookie work, you know. Back when George Bush was in office, he was out here for a fundraiser. Politicians treat L.A. like it's one giant ATM. So we block off all the streets along Overland to let the motorcade through. Only thing was, this one joker sneaked in, and he's cruising along in his red Ferrari behind all these black SUVs like he's some kind of crowned royalty. I pull him over and ticket him and he gets indignant. Informs me he's President of something or other at BMB. That he's late for a meeting. I tell this idiot it's the President of the United States, and you know what he says? He tells me so what. Says he's been President longer than Bush. Can you believe that?"

I laughed. "Sounds about right. Anything else spring to mind?"

"You mean real police work? Nah. We pull an employee over for a DUI now and then, but nothing out of the ordinary. Who are you working with over there?"

"I was hired by one of the suits. But you might know the Security Director there. Ex-LAPD. Hector Ferris."

A small scowl crossed Roberto's face. "Ferris," he said with a measure of distaste. "Sure. Worked for him for years, Broadway Division, down in the hood. Grade-A prick. He never had any of our backs. Made his mark by ratting out a few guys to Internal Affairs. The brass finally forced him into early retirement a couple of years ago. I guess he landed on his feet. Like always."

"You ever have any beef with him?"

"Me? Nah. Go along to get along. But let's just say no one threw him a party when he left."

"Interesting."

Roberto looked over at me. "So who do they have you checking out? Some exec over there?"

"Not exactly. It's someone who works for Laputa. Runs the place actually. Name's Eric Starr. Anything you can tell me about him? Something in your files, perhaps?"

"Oh, Burnside," he chuckled and glanced at his computer. "A celebrity? I believe that may cost you something."

"Geez, Roberto. I feel like I'm talking to Captain Saavedra. Do I have to promise you tickets to a Trojan football game next season? Or maybe a college basketball game? March Madness starts this week."

De Santos smiled slyly. When I first met Roberto, he used to frown at Juan Saavedra's minor indiscretions at accepting tit-for-tat seats at a ballgame or a nice steak dinner. I suppose he finally accepted the old mantra, "if you can't beat 'em, join 'em." At least he knew I was usually on the right side of the law. Or my heart was, anyway. And in this case, he knew I had a client who paid top dollar.

"I would never ask you for that," he said, offering an indignant look as phony as a three dollar bill. He smiled slightly. "I'm more of a baseball guy. The Dodgers look like they're going to have a good season. Wouldn't mind a pair of box seats for opening day."

"Done," I said.

"Okay," he said, eyeing his monitor. "Says here there was an assault charge against Starr a few years ago. Woman named Darcy Beale. Happened on site at Laputa. Security intervened, paramedics were called. Her husband had been Starr's partner, guy named Jack Beale. Report said the woman set up a meeting, wanted to talk some business. Then she said she was attacked by Mr. Starr for no apparent reason."

"Oh, right," I said. "No apparent reason. We know that happens all the time."

"Yeah, and the charges were later dropped. There was also a restraining order issued afterward. Hmmm. Apparently this was issued against Ms. Beale. By Eric Starr."

I shrugged. This sort of thing happened occasionally. Any number of things could have transpired, including the victim coming back and seeking revenge. Or Starr could have gotten a restraining order first, to try and make a statement that he was really the aggrieved party.

"And no one talked about why this happened."

"Happened behind closed doors. Only two people knew for sure. For everyone else it was hearsay."

"Anything about this Jack Beale? Died in a boating accident a few years ago."

"That one sounds familiar," he remarked, as he typed a few things into a keyboard. "Yeah, there it is. I remember now. I was still at Broadway Division. Rich guy has a few drinks, stumbles off his yacht. No one's sober enough to notice. Or maybe care. No body recovered, so no proof of any foul play. They swept the boat, but it was clean. Like I say, nothing out of the ordinary, all they found were the usual empty liquor bottles and some tiny traces of blow. More of a *National Enquirer* story than a real police investigation. Someone in the Marina worked that case. Juan might know more."

"That's it?"

"Yeah, afraid so. Sorry to lift those Dodger tickets off you so easily. My guess is you'll be back for a few more favors. Hope you don't punch anyone out this time."

"I see my reputation precedes me."

"Sure, whatever that means."

I grinned. "You know what I have to do sometimes. Part of the P.I. routine. One day maybe you'll move to the other side of the desk. At least you'll understand the drill."

"Uh-huh. So you're back working on the Westside again."

"I am. My new office is a few blocks away. Santa Monica and Sepulveda."

"Guess I'll be seeing you at a few lunch spots nearby. Hope you like sushi and ramen. It's mostly an Asian neighborhood these days."

"I don't mind. But there are still some of the old haunts left. I was just at the Apple Pan. Had lunch with an old coaching buddy from SC. He just moved over to UCLA."

"Oh, yeah?" Roberto asked. "Might that be Jay Strong?"

This time it was my turn to give a wide-eyed look. "That's right. How'd you know? You said you're not a football guy."

"I'm not. We keep getting called to Jay's place over in Brentwood. Happened a bunch of times in the past year. Domestic disturbance, usually the neighbors calling. One time his wife had to go to the ER."

"Charges dropped there, too?" I asked.

"Never filed. Wife refused. Said she fell down. How about that? Oldest story in the book."

Three

I stopped by my office, quickly handled some paperwork, and made certain I was out the door before 3:30 p.m. Rush-hour traffic on the Westside had mushroomed to the point where an ordinary ten minute drive home to Mar Vista, could easily take more than half an hour. For a brief, unthinking moment I had considered setting up an office at home. Then I remembered the reasons clients hired private investigators, and the unsavory characters who often came to visit. The idea that one of them might have contact with my three year-old son was not pleasant.

"Daddy's home!" yelled Marcus as he ran over to hug my knees. I scooped him up and raised him almost to the ceiling.

"You still like these sky hugs?"

"Yay! Again!" he demanded. I laughed and brought him down onto my shoulder for a hug before lifting him skyward a few more times. The joy radiated from his face, and from mine as well. Gail and I settled on the name Marcus as a compromise. I had wanted to name him after Bulldog Martin, my head coach at USC, who was a father figure to me at a time I desperately needed one. Gail, a budding prosecutor at the City Attorney's office, had always admired Atticus Finch, the brilliant lawyer from *To Kill A Mockingbird*. His moral fiber and unwavering sense of decency, fictional though it may have been, was a prime reason she entered the field of law. So Marcus was a name that reminded us of how we got to this special place in our lives.

"Where's Mommy?" I asked.

"At work."

"And where's Carla?"

"I dunno."

I put Marcus down, walked straight into the bedroom, and stowed my pistol in the safe. First things first. In the kitchen, Marcus's nanny, Carla, was busy fixing him a snack of sliced green apples. One of Gail's directives was that Marcus should eat healthy. Minimal candy, no soda, healthy treats. I worked hard to not give in to my baser instinct to sneak him sips of Pepsi or bites of a cheeseburger. The grandparents were another matter. Despite Gail's pleas, when her parents came over to babysit, house rules went completely out the window.

"*Hola señor*!" Carla exclaimed when she saw me.

"*Buenos tardes*," I said, depleting a good bit of my Spanish vocabulary.

"*Señora* Gail just called. She said she'd be home early for your meeting."

I frowned and checked my calendar. Nothing. Then I remembered yesterday morning. Gail had wanted a visit with a consultant, something about applications to preschool. I hadn't bothered to probe her at the time, it was one of those comments that went in one ear and out the other. Such is my new life, married with a child.

Over the past three years, my bloated paycheck had streamed enough money into our bank account as to allow me to spoil my wife and child. Growing up with a single mom, I didn't have a lot but it didn't matter much at the time. Everyone in my neighborhood was like us, scraping by. My friends and I played sports and board games, watched TV, hung around. We knew we weren't rich, but we didn't quite know what that meant.

Having been a high-profile coach at an expensive private university, I now knew full well the advantages that came with being a privileged kid. Summer trips to Europe, ski weekends to Aspen, country clubs, gated communities. That wasn't the life of the student-athletes I coached, but it did describe the reality for some of the student body at USC. And when I finally had a sizable amount of money flowing in, I wanted my family to have the type of creature comforts that were now attainable. Maybe not exclusive homes or luxury vacations, but some good things nevertheless.

We started with new cars. I surprised Gail one day with a new Audi, and got a big thrill just seeing the shocked look on her face. I treated myself to a new black Pathfinder. My 10 year-old model was showing signs of wear, and, at 140,000 miles, it was going into the shop frequently. I splurged and let a cagey salesman talk me into getting leather seats. And a moon roof. And while I rarely opened the moon roof, I just liked having it, using the accessory as something akin to a skylight.

I did need to be careful with Marcus. He had plenty of toys, but not *every* toy he wanted. Kids whose parents gave in to all requests were kids who grew up expecting life would provide them with everything they wanted. The reality is, you just don't get to have it all, life sometimes tells you no. And our saying no to Marcus was a part of being a parent. But it was hard. The ability to say yes and see the bright, sunny glow on his face often made my day.

The clicking sound of a key turning in the lock told us Gail was home. As usual, Marcus's reaction time was better than mine. Or at least more demonstrative.

"Mommy!" Marcus ran over and got the same warm greeting from Gail that he got from me, minus the sky hug.

"Hi there," she beamed, holding Marcus in one arm, her beautiful face and luminous smile never failing to strike a chord within me. "I'm glad you remembered to come home early."

"Sure," I said. No sense correcting her. "But just what is a preschool consultant?"

"Education counselor," Gail said. "My boss, Steve, raves about her. It's really just to understand about the schools in the area. Neither of us know much about it, so I figured it can't hurt to get some guidance."

"I used to work in education," I protested, the half-smile unable to stay off of my face.

"Oh, yes. I do remember. You were part of the USC faculty. But sweetie, I don't think your expertise extends to three year-olds."

"Is this necessary?" I asked.

"I don't know, to be quite honest. But Steve Reinhart said Anna Faust was the best. He told me she knows all about schools on the Westside. And when the City Attorney calls someone the best, you assume he knows what he's talking about. I thought we'd set up a meeting with her and see."

"Can't hurt to meet," I said, knowing that "the best" often carried with it an astronomic hourly rate. "Lucky thing I signed a new client today. BMB. They want me to do a background check on Eric Starr, the CEO of Laputa."

Gail smiled her electric smile. "Well, I'm glad you're getting back into the swing of things. And this sounds like an easy assignment."

"No danger at all," I joked, suddenly wondering if I had jinxed myself. Some people believe that the best way to put things in motion is to verbalize just how unlikely they would be to happen.

"There might be some things about that guy Starr in our files," Gail said. "As long as it's not an ongoing investigation, I'll see what I can learn."

"Nothing like having a mole in the City Attorney's office."

"Spouses get special treatment," she said and planted a kiss on my cheek. I had known Gail for years, but I swear I still blush when she turns her affection my way. It's a phenomena that happens when you've waited a very long time for the girl of your dreams to appear.

We cleaned up some of the toys Marcus had spread out along the living room floor. I had bought him a bag of a hundred polished rocks, and he had chosen to lay them out in order, ranked by his favorite colors. When Marcus objected vehemently to my messing up his work, I pulled out my iPhone and took a photo of it, telling him he would now have a record of this ranking forever. That managed to appease him, and he went off to play with something else. Our black cocker spaniel, Chewy, wandered in with her tail wagging as she offered a great big yawn. Having been happily napping in the other room, she was curious enough to come see what the fuss was all about. She sniffed around, didn't sense any food nearby, so she went off into a corner and curled up to groom herself. We were the happy suburban family.

The doorbell rang, and Gail let Anna Faust in. She looked a little younger than me, despite having gray hair that flowed down past her shoulders. She wore an olive green sweater with a yellow scarf that came down across the front of her torso. She was attractive and bubbly and gave off a professional demeanor.

"What a lovely home!" she declared in what might have been a finishing-school accent. "My husband and I, our first home was in Mar Vista."

"Where do you live now?" I asked.

"Hey, that's nosy," Gail poked at me. "You're off duty."

"Oh, it's all right," she said. "We live in Beverly Hills."

"A far cry from Mar Vista."

"Oh no, not really," she said. "It's still L.A. after all."

We sat down, poured some decaf and let Anna Faust begin to indoctrinate us into the curious world of being L.A. parents. Our conversations with other parents would invariably drift to the issue of schools, which ones we were looking at and where we were thinking of applying. There were apparently some finely honed strategies for getting kids into good schools, be they public or private. And Marcus had just turned three in January.

"You're a little behind," Anna observed, stirring some cream into her cup. "Most parents start the process when their child is two years old."

"The process?" I asked, my eyebrows starting to arch, and a small, throbbing pain beginning to take hold in the back of my head.

"Oh yes," she said. "There is most definitely a process for kids. It begins with the right preschool. You want a feeder school that can get your child admitted into a top elementary school. One that sends their students to the best high schools. Students from those high schools are the ones the elite colleges will give the most consideration. It's all about getting into the best college."

"Of course," I said weakly. How stupid of me to not know this.

"So," Gail said, her brow frowning. "You say we're behind in this ... process?"

"Unfortunately, yes," she said. "Many preschools begin admitting children at age two. They start with a few half-days a week. It's a transitional program. When they're three, they begin formal preschool every day."

My head really began to hurt now. I turned to Gail, who was focused and involved and seemingly happy enough to take the lead. Marcus sat in a corner, playing with a couple of toy Matchbox cars. Chewy yawned again and curled into a ball for a nap. I felt like going outside and shooting baskets at the hoop I had hung above the garage. That would not go over well with these women however, especially the one I woke up with every morning.

"So what are our options?" Gail asked.

"Well, it's a little difficult to be sure, but I think there will be some spots opening in the fall. There's always a few children that will leave, transfer to another preschool or move out of the area. Fortunately, I am well acquainted with a number of preschool directors. I'm sure I can steer you to the one that's right for your son. The fact that the City Attorney recommended you is a huge plus. I'm happy to help anyone Steve Reinhardt recommends."

"That's nice of you," I said, now clearly worrying how much this preferential treatment would cost us. Being a former police officer, I was accustomed to sensing there was a price for every favor and a hidden agenda behind every good deed. It was a skeptic's mindset, an occupational hazard I needed to navigate when mixing business with our personal life.

"My pleasure. I love helping young couples. May I ask what your occupations are?"

"I used to coach football at USC," I said, allowing a hint of pride to enter the timbre of my voice.

"Oh, how marvelous!" she exclaimed. "You're something of a celebrity then!"

"Minor celebrity," I said, the pride starting to wane as I thought of how to describe my current position. Telling her I was paid to investigate the private goings-on of senior executives, and sometimes engage in thug-like activities would not endear me to an exclusive pre-school, or most civilized human beings.

"And what are you doing now?" she asked.

"I own my own business," I managed, trying to puff out my chest. "It's something of a research agency."

"And," Gail said, jumping in, "I'm a prosecutor. I'm sure you know I work in the City Attorney's office."

"Well," Anna said. "Two polished professionals. That's exactly what these preschools look for in parents. I don't see anything hindering your application."

At that point, Marcus grew bored of playing with his toy cars. He noticed Chewy snoozing away and decided it would be the ideal time to reach out and pull her tail. And before we could even sense what was happening, he walked over and gave it a good, hard tug. Chewy reacted with a shrieking bark, jumped up, and glared at him over the indignity of being violated. Thankfully, she didn't growl at him. Instead, she began to take a step or two backwards as she saw the shocked, wide-eyed look he gave her in return. I walked over, picked Marcus up, and carried him to the couch.

"Not a good thing to pull a dog's tail," I told him.

"Uh-huh," he said. "I'm sorry."

"It's okay," I said and stroked his hair. "All part of the growing-up process. You're getting to be a bigger boy and curiosity is part of that."

"Curi ... huh?" he said.

"Curiosity," I repeated. "It means being interested in something new."

"Ah, yes," Gail said and turned to Anna. "Sorry about that. Kids do the darndest things."

Anna shrugged. "I've seen worse, believe me. But you two are quite involved parents. That's a good thing. Your son will be fine. Your dog, er, may need to find her own space."

"Hmmm," I observed, before deciding to pose the question that was often posed to me. "Do you mind if I ask what your fee is?"

"Of course not. I charge five hundred dollars an hour."

"I see," I managed, with as much of a smile as I could muster, one that would hopefully imply that this was a perfectly reasonable price that any normal working stiff would gladly fork over. While Anne probably didn't work an 8-hour day, her hourly rate was far more than what Gail and I made combined.

"Were you always in this field?" Gail asked.

"No, it began as a personal interest. I have three children. With public schools in L.A. being what they are, I started learning more about the private schools. After a while, I began giving advice to other parents. Pretty soon I was able to charge for it. And after a while I was making more money at this than in the career I studied for. And enjoying it a lot more, too."

"What did you do before this?" I asked.

"I used to head up Human Resources for a few local companies. The last one was Laputa, the internet site. I'm sure you've heard of it."

I nodded and tried to keep my jaw from dropping. In my mind I could see pieces of a jigsaw puzzle floating around. None seemed to fit together.

*

The next morning came early, like it always does for me. When I lived in my Santa Monica apartment, the downstairs neighbor, Ms. Linzmeier, often managed to wake me before 5:30 a.m. Now it was the planes taking off from nearby Santa Monica Airport that jolted me out of bed. Gail invariably slept as if the roar from the jets were nothing more than the soft whispers of a passing breeze. Lately there had been rumors the airport might be shuttered. If so, I'll probably need to finally buy myself an alarm clock.

I combed through the Internet and learned more about Eric Starr. He had grown up in the comfortable confines of Irvine, a planned community in Orange County, about forty miles south of L.A. Graduated in three years from UC-Irvine, he started working at Hayes, a company that builds computers. Starr met Jack Beale there and the two of them formed Laputa, which quickly became successful. After Beale drowned, Starr gained full control of Laputa. The company continued to grow, and Eric was hailed as a business genius.

My search finished when Marcus woke up, and Gail followed soon afterward. I played with Marcus while Gail got ready for work, and as she hurried out the door, we agreed to talk more about preschools this weekend. Not a conversation I was looking forward to. I spent some time on the floor with Marcus, trying to teach him to play Go Fish. Ultimately we decided it was more fun to take the deck of cards and toss each one individually across the room, attempting to land them standing up, leaning against the wall. He was winning 3-2 in our game of Leaners when Carla arrived. This freed me up to go to work, but not before Marcus made me promise he would get the opportunity to beat me once again.

The drive down to Irvine took about 45 minutes, the traffic was remarkably clear. Most of the congestion was on the northbound side of the San Diego Freeway, as cars jockeyed to get up to West L.A. a minute or two quicker. As I arrived in Irvine, I searched for a Starbuck's, but all I found was an IHOP. I ordered a watery coffee to go and, winced with every sip. Sitting in my Pathfinder, I watched some local homemakers and retirees enter a Whole Foods across the street. The morning was bright, pretty and serene, and I was presented with a perfect picture of suburbia. Maybe near-perfect. I drank about half of my coffee before walking over to a trash bin to dump the remaining swill. In some neighborhoods, it would have been perfectly fine to pour the contents onto the asphalt parking lot. Here in Irvine, such a demonstration might be tantamount to intentionally staining someone's living room carpet.

I drove up Ridgeline Drive and found the street on which Eric Starr grew up, where his parents still lived. This was in the upscale Turtle Rock section of Irvine, lined with one beautiful home after another. Irvine was a city of carefully detailed neighborhoods, designed by urban planners who wanted to create a world in which every home looked perfect. And looked the same. The street names were called Moonrise, Moonlight, Moonshine, Moonbeam and a few others that appeared to be specifically designed to confuse visitors. There were no front yards, no cars parked in driveways, everything was neat and orderly. Only the approved colors of the houses differed, although the pale blue, pale gray and pale beige were, I decided, not exceptionally different from one another. They were just pale.

The first doors I knocked on bore little fruit. Some owners were not at home, some had moved in well after Eric Starr had moved out. But mostly, the people I met just didn't want to talk. The person next door to Starr's parents said he had lived there for two years and had not even met Cindy and Benjamin Starr, much less Eric. Finally, I struck pay dirt. The woman across the street had been well-acquainted with the Starr family for years. And she was all too willing to speak about them.

"They're something else," said Margaret Walsh, a 60-ish, bird-boned woman wearing a green flowing skirt, her reddish hair piled into a bun that sat atop her head.

"How so?" I asked.

"That family's the perfect American success story. Until you pull back the covers and take a look under the hood."

I decided not to shine a spotlight on the mixed metaphors. "Really," I said conversationally.

"Oh, yes. The father goes off traveling for weeks on end. Comes back periodically, at odd times of the day and night. I think he even might be home right now if you want to talk to him. But he's usually flying around the world, making a ton of money. He has to, his trophy wife spends it non-stop."

"Did you know Eric?"

"Sure. Quite the meteoric rise. Well, with an absentee dad and an self-obsessed mom, how could he not be?" she remarked caustically. "Hey, the kid was very bright, I'll give him that. Near-genius IQ, to hear some people tell it. My son was in the same year as him in school, that's how we know. But Eric only worked hard when he wanted to. Got A's in some classes and D's in others. Probably could have gone to Harvard if he applied himself. I hear his father had to pull some strings to even enroll him at UC-Irvine. Just down the road."

"Got him his first job too, I hear."

"Sure. At Hayes. No one else would hire him. Isn't that ironic? The boy who can't find a job working for anyone except his father winds up launching an empire."

"What kind of a kid was he?" I asked. "Growing up."

"Not the kind I'd want my kids hanging around. Nasty, selfish, unforgiving. Quite the partier, too. You could smell the pot smoke coming out of their hot tub at night. Our youngest went over there a few times. Fortunately they didn't hit it off."

"Did the Starrs have any other kids?"

"One. Younger son, Lanny. Still lives at home. Dad got him into UC-Irvine too, but he flunked out. Eric got him a job up at Laputa when he was launching it. But he fired Lanny after a while."

"Fired his own brother?"

"Yeah," she cackled. "Can you believe that? Tells you all you need to know about Eric. Now the youngest just sits on the couch playing video games. What a waste."

"Can you tell me more about the dad?"

Margaret hesitated and looked behind me. "Maybe you should ask him yourself. Here he comes."

around the corner. A white patrol car with "Orange Security" on the door roared up and jerked to a stop in front of Margaret Walsh's house. The driver parked on the wrong side of the street. A khaki-clad uniformed officer got out of the cruiser, spoke with Starr for a moment, and then approached me.

"Please state your business, sir," he demanded, his voice crisp and confident.

"You know, they have street sweeping here today. You might want to move your vehicle. I'd hate for it to get towed. I might even have to call it in myself."

"Let me worry about that, smart guy. Again, state your business."

"I'm having a chat with one of my oldest and dearest friends," I said and turned to Mrs. Walsh. "Isn't that right, Margaret?"

Margaret Walsh laughed. "Sure," she said. "My old pal. What was your name again?"

The officer gave me a terse look. "I'm going to have to ask you to leave the premises, sir."

I turned back to Margaret. "You wouldn't back up my story? For shame."

She shrugged. "You seem like a decent guy. But I have to know you a little better before I can lie for you."

"Understood," I sighed, recognizing there were things about the suburbs I would need to learn. I turned back to the security guard. "Sorry. I'm not ready to leave yet. Free country and all that. You know."

"I'm not going to ask you again, sir," he warned me.

"Well that's a relief."

"You're asking for trouble."

"Won't be the first time," I sighed. "I suppose I should ask what you're going to do if I don't leave voluntarily. Or pleasantly."

The security officer reached over with his right hand and pointed to a can of pepper spray strapped to his belt. "That enough motivation for you to take off, smart guy?"

"You always carry your deodorant around with you?"

Jerking the can out of the holster with his right hand, he quickly reached over with his left to remove the safety latch. Using pepper spray in this type of situation was wholly unwarranted, but that wouldn't stop my eyes from stinging badly for the next few hours. In the end, the security guard might just get a rebuke for being overzealous. I didn't have a lot of time to think, but letting him spray me was not in my best interests. I reared back and hit him with a left hook between the eyes, and he stumbled and fell onto the lawn. Still holding the can of pepper spray, he went back to struggling to remove the safety.

I took two quick steps and kicked his right hand. The can dropped onto the grass, and after grimacing in pain for a second, he went to grab it yet again, this time with his left hand. Some people just didn't know when to cut their losses. I finally reached down and yanked it out of his hand.

"I'm calling 911," he yelped, in a voice that was now more whine than swagger.

I stared at him in disbelief. "Do I have to beat your phone out of you, too?"

He began to reach into his jacket pocket, so I reached into mine first. I assumed he'd grab his phone, but you never know when someone is armed with a lethal weapon. I drew my .38 and pointed it at him.

"Keep those hands where I can see them," I growled. "Take your hand out of your jacket. And I mean now. Do it."

He slowly removed his hand and eyed me. "You're in a lot of trouble, mister. You don't know what you've just done."

"Sure I do. I engaged in self-defense with an amateur thug wearing a stupid uniform."

He looked at me nervously, and it seemed like the gears inside his brain were working overtime. It felt like he was trying to decide what he should do next, and whether it was worth getting shot over a few nasty words. I solved the problem for him by reaching into his pocket and taking his phone.

Walking over to Margaret, I kept one eye on the guard as I handed her a business card. "Mrs. Walsh, give me a call if you think of anything else. Anything at all."

She stared at me in awe. "All right," she said, with quite a bit of hesitation in her voice. "Talking by phone might be a better idea. All things considered."

My gun was pointed down at the ground as I walked past the security officer. His body was frozen in place on the lawn, but he watched me carefully. Benjamin Starr watched me carefully as well. I glanced at Starr and pointed a finger at him.

"My business here isn't finished," I said.

"It is as far as I'm concerned," Starr responded, his voice a little shaky despite the bluster of his words.

"Your concerns don't interest me," I said, shaking my head as I walked to my Pathfinder. Jumping in quickly, I turned over the engine and pulled onto the street. As I sped from the scene, I threw the guard's pepper spray and cell phone out of the window and onto the sidewalk.

*

I drove quickly away from Moonrise Drive, flew down Ridgeline and then jumped onto the San Diego freeway heading north. I kept one eye on the rear-view mirror to see if anyone was tailing me. No one was. After about 10 miles, satisfied there were no police cars in hot pursuit, I stopped for a mediocre cheeseburger at a chain restaurant. It paled in comparison to the burgers they serve at the Apple Pan. The restaurant had at least a dozen TVs mounted throughout the room. Most were tuned to ESPN. I'm sure there were better places to eat in Orange County, I just didn't happen to know of any. I also didn't have a contact in the Irvine P.D., which meant I had no leverage if the security guard had indeed called 911. I did know Juan Saavedra now lived in nearby Mission Viejo, but that wouldn't prevent an overnight stay in the Irvine jail. And I didn't think my attorney spouse would be pleased at the thought of having to pull strings in another jurisdiction to extricate her combative husband from the clink. But it did seem to be worthwhile to go and have a chat with Juan.

Before driving back to the Westside, I placed a call to the Purdue Division. Juan was in the field, but his assistant told me he would be leaving early today on personal business. A little probing with her revealed that Juan's son had a basketball game in Gardena later that afternoon. The CIF playoffs were starting, and like any proud parent, Juan hated to miss a game. Short of a major tactical alert, the Captain would be knocking off early today.

The drive to Gardena didn't take long, but it was still early afternoon. Later in the day, the freeways would be gridlocked. I made a few phone calls, scanned the internet on my iPad, and mostly sought out ways to kill a few hours. I parked in the lot at Junipero Serra High school, and took a walk around the neighborhood. Gardena was a blue-collar community in the South Bay, a mixture of many ethnicities, from Hispanic to Pan-Asian to African-American, and could easily serve as a microcosm for L.A. itself.

Some people called L.A. the great experiment. Los Angeles was a cosmopolitan area that attracted people from every corner of the world. It wasn't necessarily a melting pot though, it was more of a salad bowl. People often stayed with their own group, but L.A. was also one of the most tolerant places on earth. You could find your niche, and these days, you normally didn't get bothered because you looked or acted differently. That hadn't always been true, but L.A. had evolved. It was hard to say whether this experiment could be duplicated elsewhere. L.A. might just be a little too unique.

I walked back onto the school grounds and strolled over to the football field. I had visited this campus countless times over the past three years, Serra was a showcase for some of the best prep football players in the country, and recruiting them into the Trojan family was a top priority. When he was head coach, Johnny declared he wanted to build an invisible fence around Southern California, corralling the biggest talent and enrolling them at USC. That meant frequent visits and frequent smiles. I quickly learned my role as an assistant coach began with recruiting top players. And that also meant becoming a salesman, a job I had some difficulty morphing into.

High school basketball games are normally free, except during the playoffs. The tired-looking parent volunteer at the gym entrance collected a ten dollar bill from me, before engaging in a spirited argument with a pair of teenagers. They had forgotten their IDs and the parent aide wouldn't let them take advantage of the five dollar student discount. The kids started to walk away in disgust. I called them back.

"Pay your five dollars. I'll pick up the difference."

"Hey, man. You don't have to do that," one of them said, a light-skinned African-American kid with the hint of a moustache. He was wearing a bright blue hoodie with the school name emblazoned across the front.

"It's okay. Serra's been pretty good to us. I used to coach football at USC. I know some of the people here."

"Oh, yeah?" he asked, eyes widening. "Did you coach Marquis Lee?"

"No, I coached defensive backs. But Marquis was

before my time. You know him?"

"My older brother was in his class. Hey, thanks. You checking out one of our guys for basketball?"

I smiled what might have been a sad smile. "I'm just seeing a friend. His son's playing for St. Luke's."

The kids paid their five dollar fees, and I handed some more money to the parent volunteer, along with my disapproving look which was mostly ignored. I knew there were rules to follow, but not giving a teenager a student discount when he's obviously a student stretched the boundaries of reasonable behavior.

The Serra gym had been a mainstay in local high school sports for many years. The stands were pull-out bleachers that were rickety and proved challenging to climb up. They were half-empty and I could only imagine what the weight of a full house might do to them. They creaked with every step I took. I scanned the crowd and it didn't take long to find the ruddy face and close-cropped silver hair that belonged to a certain LAPD Captain. I navigated over to him.

"Juan Saavedra. Funny running into you here."

The deep-set brown eyes focused on me, curious for a moment before recognition set in. "Well, looky here. If it isn't L.A.'s most famous former football coach. You still scouting talent or just come by to give my boy's team some moral support?"

"Oh, you know me, Juan. I just like a good game to watch."

"More like you need a favor. This game won't be close," he observed.

I raised my eyebrows. "How so?"

He pointed to the two teams that had just come out onto the polished floor. Every player on the Serra team was at least 6'3" and some reached 6'9". All were lean and athletic. By contrast, the tallest player on St. Luke's might have been 6'4", with most of the squad closer to 6'0" tall. Or shorter. In football, there is no substitute for speed. In basketball, it's length.

"Roberto tell you I left early? He said you were sniffing around the division yesterday."

"It wasn't Roberto who gave you up," I said. "My ears are everywhere."

"Ah, I forgot who I was dealing with. You planning on giving my assistant tickets to a game, also?"

"Maybe an iced Frappucino."

"She'd like that better," Juan said. "So tell me what you're working on. Got a new client already?"

"Yeah. BMB. Some background work."

Juan looked at me. "BMB?" he said with a chuckle. "I suppose they'll pay you well. But Roberto mentioned something about your looking into a cold case with the founder of Laputa. Drowned off of the Marina."

"Co-founder, name's Jack Beale. I'm actually looking into his business partner. But I guess Beale was high-profile. Your guys work that case?"

"We didn't work it, but I remember it. Ripe for a TV movie. Millionaire gets drunk, falls into the ocean, and no one on the boat notices until it's too late. Everyone on board was either a big shot at Laputa or had a spouse that was. They all pretty much kept their mouths shut. Solving that one would have been tough for Agatha Christie."

"Think there was anything there beyond an accident?" I asked.

"Maybe. But when no one is talking and no evidence exists, you can't do much. And the guy that benefited the most, Eric Starr, he wasn't even on the boat."

"Speaking of Starr, anything you can share about him?"

"Arrogant bastard, but that's all I really could gather. He may have had a thing with his partner's wife, who knows. They had some animosity, that's for sure. Why the interest?"

"Search committee at BMB asked me to look into Starr. Hiring decision. Confidential, of course," I said with a wink.

"Interesting. I'll keep that to myself," he grinned.

"What about his family? I understand Starr grew up in Irvine. Near where you live now. Know anything?"

"Oh, sure. I know everyone who lives in south Orange County. Must be a million people there now."

"I'd settle for a contact on the Irvine P.D."

"That I might be able to help you on. Let me go through my file at the office."

We turned our attention to the game. Serra won the opening tip and proceeded to score the first 12 points at a rapid clip. Juan's son made a couple of three-point baskets to shave the lead to 12-6 before Serra went on another tear. They scored 8 more unanswered points, and then a thundering, two-handed slam dunk from the Serra center brought the crowd to its feet. A weary-looking St.

Luke's coach signaled for a timeout.

"Not a real fair matchup for a playoff game," I commented. "Your kid's team is going to get boat-raced."

"First round is always like this. St. Luke's won their conference, but it's a weak one. And besides, we're more of a football school."

"Your son play?"

"I wanted him to. But my better half was worried about concussions. Her line in the sand. So we did this thing that married couples do. It's called compromise. He can play any sport except football."

I thought about this. Last year I made a few jokes about Marcus joining a Pop Warner football league when he came of age. In the world of Pop Warner, the minimum age turned out to be five years old. Gail gave me a look that silently said this was a subject in dire need of discussion. There were risks in everything, and I had seen kids get hurt in all sports, including non-contact ones. Basketball players can take a tumble and land head first onto an unforgiving hardwood floor. Same with volleyball, they play on the same court, and kids sometimes dive for balls. Tennis players can get severe tendonitis in the elbow or knee. Baseball players can get beaned. No matter how many precautions a parent takes, a kid playing sports runs the risk of injury. Usually it's not serious. Once in a while it is.

"I think playing a team sport is a positive thing for a kid," I said. "If it's a good team with a good coach, the experience can last a lifetime."

"The good coach part, yeah. You think you'll miss it?"

I sighed and looked towards the other side of the gym. A stage was set up behind the team benches, since the school used the gym as a theater or an auditorium when it wasn't being used for basketball. Back in the day, multipurpose structures were common. Today, everyone wants their own space. In one exclusive private high school in the Valley, a wealthy parent contributed to the building of an Olympic-sized swimming pool on the campus. He thought his son had the potential to win a gold medal. In the end, the kid barely made the school swim team.

"I miss the guys," I said. "That was always the driving force for me. I'll admit I wasn't the best coach in the world, but I wasn't the worst, either. I was trying to motivate the players to be the best athletes, the best competitors. And mostly, the best people they could be."

"SC always gets a lot of talent."

"Sure. But the kids all came in thinking they'd go on to the pros. Every one of them were stars in high school. College is different."

"Next level is always tougher. In everything."

"Yup. Especially the NFL. It's uber-competitive. So a lot of the players I coached weren't going to make it big in pro football. A few of them might, some could win a starting job for a while, a few more could hang on as backup or as a special teams player. I kept telling them to get their degrees. They all wanted a shot at the NFL, but the odds are steep. I kept reminding them that pro football is a really bad job that just pays really well."

"How did that go over?"

I shrugged. "When kids think they have a shot at making millions, they don't recognize the costs involved. Most would do anything to make it to the NFL. So my approach was to use that drive to get them in top condition, mentally and physically. I didn't focus so much on the opponent each week. I just tried to get them to play up to their ability. I figured that would translate into success of some kind in life after football."

"I guess it worked. SC got to the national title game two years ago."

"We did. Close game with Texas, but a tough loss. Everyone took it hard. It's a different world today. If you lose a championship game, you're simply a loser. Doesn't matter if you were undefeated all season. One team wins the title, everyone else is a failure. I didn't like that part."

"You were always different," Juan mused.

"And that's one of the reasons I'm not that sorry I'm out of that life. Not that I had a lot of options in the end. Any new coaching job would have meant moving from L.A. I like it here. It's home."

We turned back to the court. With the timeout over, St. Luke's ran a pick-and-roll and scored an uncontested basket. Then Serra took off on another spurt. By halftime the score was 49-16. Juan didn't look upset about this. In fact, he said, Serra would probably put in their second stringers and his son might get to play against kids of his own caliber.

At that point, Juan's cell phone rang. His face grew tighter as he listened. He asked the basic questions, who, when, where, how. Then he gave instructions as to which squads to deploy. He hung up the phone and looked at me.

"I have to go," he said grimly, looking for a path down the bleachers.

"Duty calls?"

"Yeah. And it's funny your being down here with me now. You might want to tag along on this one."

"All right. What happened?" I asked, not looking forward to what I was about to hear.

"That was Robbery-Homicide. We lost one of our own today. Well, he used to be on the job, anyway."

"Did I work with him?" I asked, as I followed his steps.

"Oh, I think you know him," Juan replied as he began to carefully climb down toward the gym floor. "Hector Ferris. Outside chance it might have been a hit-and-run accident. But more likely someone was targeting him."

Four

The Rancho Park neighborhood is a community best known for its golf course. At one time, Rancho Park was included in the PGA Tour, but that was many decades ago, having been nudged aside by the tonier Riviera Country Club in the Palisades. Nestled beside the wealthier Cheviot Hills enclave, Rancho Park was what passes for middle class on the Westside of L.A. Middle class is a fluid term, though; homes in Rancho Park often sell for what would be considered outlandish prices in the rest of the country. And even with that, some pay a ridiculous sum just to buy a house, tear it down, and construct a bigger one in its place.

Hector Ferris lived a block south of Pico, in the shadow of the Westside Pavilion, on a sleepy street where not much drama ever occurred. His house was on a particularly quiet block, shaded by long rows of jacaranda trees. For about a month or so each spring, the trees would bloom with lavender flowers. The delicate petals would float down and create a purple dusting atop the green lawns during much of May and June. But on this early evening in mid-March, the streets were lined instead with police cars, the lawns covered only with grim-faced uniformed officers.

Access to the street was blocked off by orange cones, and yellow tape had been hastily strung to cordon off the crime scene. One of the uniforms approached me and told me this was not a place for visitors, but a brief conversation with Juan allowed me to be waved on in. Roberto De Santos was standing in the street a few yards away from the victim, the body covered indelicately with an off-white sheet. Roberto was listening to one of the investigators explain why this wasn't an accident.

"No skid marks, that's the tell," said a long, thin man with unruly hair that looked like it hadn't been combed all day. He wore a blue windbreaker, unzipped, and waved his arms about as he spoke. "Everything we need is right there on the street. You just have to know what to look for."

"Go on, Lew," Roberto said.

"If this had been an accident," he continued, "skid marks would show on the pavement, right near the initial impact. They would indicate the driver tried to apply the brakes before the crash. None of that is evident. No sign of braking whatsoever."

"What else?"

"Follow me," he directed, and we walked 30 yards up the block. He stopped and dramatically pointed down at the ground. A pair of fresh black streaks were embedded into the asphalt, the marks about six feet apart, the distance that separated two front tires. "This is where the driver started out."

"How do you know for sure?" someone asked.

The investigator sniffed and gestured at the pair of black patches.

"This might look like a skid mark to the untrained observer. It's actually what we call an acceleration scuff mark. You know that old saying, 'leave rubber on the road'? Well, this is what it looks like. This is where they gunned the engine and took off. Jackrabbit start. Whoever did this was waiting for the right moment. When they saw the victim enter the street, they floored it. Couldn't have been more than 20 feet away from him, we see bloodstains at the initial impact. Blunt-force trauma. Then it just continues for a good 75 feet as the body dragged underneath the vehicle. Probably hooked on by a piece of clothing. The manhole cover finally extricated the body. Lucky thing for the driver."

"Meaning if the body was still attached to the vehicle ... " Roberto started.

"Then the vehicle couldn't have been driven much further. And the driver would have been stuck there. Could have gotten out and ran, I suppose, but a getaway on foot is far more difficult. And we would have had the license plate. May have been stolen, but it would have been a place to begin. At least there was one person who saw this happen from a distance. Said it was an SUV. Thought it was dark green."

Roberto wiped his face. "Okay. Thanks," he said. "Keep digging on this, see if we can get a match on the type of tires. Could narrow it down a little."

The tall man in the blue windbreaker shrugged. "Sure."

Roberto started walking away and then noticed me. "Burnside. Need to speak with you. Glad you're here."

"I don't get told that very often."

Roberto managed a dry half-smile before walking off.

"Stick around. I have some assignments to give out. But I want to talk to you."

I waited a while as Roberto weaved slowly through the crowd of officers. Across the street, neighbors stood in front of their homes, huddling together in groups of three and four. I noticed one man standing by himself, rocking back and forth as if he were listening to a tune in his head. In his hand was a can of something, neatly encased in a yellow insulated-foam holder. The holder was designed to keep the can cold, but it also masked what he was drinking. He wore dark green cargo shorts and a black t-shirt promoting a local soccer team. If the man was drinking alcohol, he might be loose-lipped enough to reveal something interesting. And while the detectives would hardly approve of my interviewing potential witnesses before they did, I also recognized his tipsiness might not last long.

"Quite a scene here, huh?" I said, smelling that he had beer breath.

"You betcha. I can't wait for Eyewitness News to show up. I want to be on TV."

"You knew Hector?"

"Sure, he lived two doors down. Hector was the neighborhood asshole. Every block's got one."

"Oh, yeah?" I asked, wondering how this conversation would play out on Eyewitness News.

"Yup. Anyone got out of line, Hector was in their face. He once came over and told me I couldn't park on my own lawn. Guess he figured since he was LAPD he could push people around."

"Bet you didn't like that."

"Damn straight I didn't. It's my property. I should be able to park where I want to."

"Sure," I said agreeably. "You have any other problems with Hector?"

"Ah, he was just a typical cop. Telling people keep the noise down, don't water your lawn in the middle of the day. Stupid stuff," he said, peering at me. "Hey. You a cop?"

"Not me," I said, holding up my hand. "I just saw the commotion driving by."

"Yeah, well, Hector was a douche. No surprise he pissed someone off. Plus, he liked to strut. Dude drove a BMW, even bragged about this Rolex he got last Christmas. What a bunch of bull."

"How's that?"

"The BMW was 20 years old. And I took a look at the watch of his. It was a knockoff."

"How do you know?"

"Oh, uh, my cousin works in the business. Jewelry and, uh, that kind of stuff. He said there was a way to tell with a Rolex. The second hand is supposed to make a sweeping motion. Moves cleanly. Hector's moved a second and then stopped, moved a second and then stopped. You can also tell by the date magnifier, that little glass bubble on the side of the face. It's expensive as hell, so the counterfeiters don't put in the real thing. That's how you can tell a knockoff. It also has a loud ticking sound when it's fake."

"Interesting," I said, making a mental note to check

this out later, and wondering what my new friend did for a living. "So Hector wasn't an honest guy."

"Like I said, he was an asshole. He just liked to show off."

"Hmmm. So you think it was someone in the neighborhood who did this?"

The man took a swig from his can and looked off in the distance, pondering this intriguing question with great thought. He took a deep breath and weighed the options. Finally, after a lengthy pause from which I hoped some well thought-out nugget of insight might arise, he spoke.

"Nah," he blurted, wrinkling his nose in the process. "I don't think so."

"You seem quite certain of that."

"Yeah, well, Hector was a jerk, but I don't see anyone around here doing this just because he gave them a hard time. And everyone knew he was a cop with a gun. Or former cop. He didn't let on to the neighbors that he left the LAPD. I knew, though. The mailman used to screw up regularly and deliver his mail to me by mistake. I once got his pension check, in fact. Jeez, but retired cops got a good deal."

"You opened his mail?"

"Sure, why not. It's my tax dollars, ain't it?"

I blinked a few times. "Right," I said, not feeling in the mood to argue with logic like his. "So someone ran him down. Who do you think did it?"

"Could've been anyone."

This was getting me nowhere. I suddenly had an idea. A long time ago I had heard a psychologist suggest a technique to allow kids to open up, and I wondered if it would work on inebriates. I raised up my fist as if I were holding a microphone.

"Let's practice your on-camera interview," I teased. "Pretend I'm a reporter with Eyewitness News. Okay sir, tell us in your own words what you think happened here tonight."

He chuckled and took another swallow of beer "Well, I'll tell you," he bellowed, obviously enjoying the role I had cast him in. "His name was Hector Ferris and he used to work in law enforcement. So naturally he was a man with a lot of enemies."

"Any you know of, sir?" I asked, moving my pretend microphone closer to his mouth.

"Not personally, no. But he was acting very nervous this week. I think he was worried about something."

I stared at him. "Worried?"

"He looked worried, yes. Something's been on his mind lately. Didn't seem the same."

"What's your theory about what happened?" I asked, starting to speculate what he might say if a real camera actually were pointed at him.

"Well, you know, Ferris put a lot of people away. Bad people. it's easy to think they hatched a revenge scheme when they were in the can. But that's the easy answer. Crooks usually scrap that sort of idea once they get released from prison. They're not crazy about going back in."

I looked at him curiously. This was a topic he might have actually thought through.

"Oh, no?"

"Nope," he continued, "I think whoever did this knew Hector. Knew him well. There's an old saying that to know someone is to love them. Well, in Hector's case, to know him is to want to kill him. I would think it was someone who knew him pretty well. Maybe someone he used to work with at the LAPD. I heard he ticked a lot of cops off."

I continued to gaze at him for a long moment before I slowly lowered my pretend microphone. I made a mental note to tell Gail she might need to revise her comment from yesterday. Children, as well as drunks, say the darndest things.

*

It took Roberto over an hour to walk back to me, and he and Juan approached me together. By that time, many of the neighbors had gone inside. Real police activity was exciting only at first. After that, the process offered very little in the way of action, and was not good entertainment value. The homicide detectives would spend the next few hours going door-to-door, interviewing residents for any morsel of information they might have. A little while ago, Hector's wife drove up. After she prodded every officer who would look at her, one finally directed her to Juan, who took her aside and broke the news. Her reaction was to put her hand over mouth and stand like that for at least ten minutes, motionless to the point of appearing almost catatonic.

"Telling the spouse is tough," Juan said. "Toughest

part of the job."

"They're normally the first one you suspect."

"Generally. But this was premeditated. Not some heat-of-the-moment crime. The driver had to be lying in wait. Doesn't mean it wasn't the spouse. Or someone she could have hired. But nothing we have indicates any marital strife. At least nothing out of the ordinary."

"Meaning?"

"Every couple fights about something. Usually it's about money. Inez is in too much shock to remember anything. My sixth sense tells me she's not involved here."

"So what other avenues are you going down?"

"Well, maybe," Juan said, "that leads us to you."

I gaped at him. "Oh. The suspicious private eye. Of course, I have a rock-solid alibi. Being in the company of an LAPD Captain at the time of the incident. Unless you have trouble recalling where you were earlier."

"Knock it off, will you?" Juan said, a little irritated. "It's going to be a long night here. And whatever we might have thought of Ferris, he was still a brother."

"Okay. So how does this lead to me?"

"You spoke with Hector yesterday. In his office. Let's talk some more about that conversation over at BMB."

"Let's."

"You knew Ferris from when we were at the Broadway Division."

"Knew him," I said. "Not well. But well enough to not trust him."

"Yeah," Juan sighed. "No one did. He'd was in good with I.A."

I.A. stood for Internal Affairs, the department that looked into police actions. It was mostly routine work, officer-involved shootings, but they also investigated cops who might be on the take, committing fraud or simply violating rules. I.A. was widely loathed among the rank-and-file, and their crew often looked to investigate any officer who gave off even a whiff of impropriety. Within the Broadway Division, which was in a poverty-stricken, drug-infested area off of 77th Street in South L.A., many officers suspected Ferris of feeding info to I.A. Ferris was an average cop who quickly moved up to the rank of Lieutenant, which meant he had friends in certain places. As well as enemies among everyone else.

"I heard Hector retired a couple of years ago," I said. "Forced out."

"I can't discuss those details. But maybe you can discuss what you talked about with Hector. We already know about the Eric Starr investigation. What else?"

I shrugged. "Something about sexual harassment. I guess it happens a lot over at BMB. Hector wouldn't go into details, but I got the distinct feeling that was a big part of his job."

"Any names?" Roberto asked.

I considered this. There might be nothing to the Patty Muckenthaler situation. And then again, there might be something. Withholding information from the police was generally not a good idea. Unless I was working in their best interest. And the fact that I was already involved here meant I had access to people who might speak more openly with me than with the police. If my conversations didn't pan out, I could always pass the names to Juan and Roberto afterward. I thought about the ethics of this and decided to think about something else. What to have for breakfast tomorrow was sounding more appealing.

"None that I recall," I told him.

"Oh, he doesn't recall," Juan parroted. "Not that he doesn't have anything to share, he just isn't able to share it with us just yet."

"That's a little harsh, my friend," I said.

"You want to talk harsh? If you're withholding evidence, then don't think that tickets to a ballgame are going to buy your way out."

Roberto looked down at the ground and whistled softly. I got the feeling he was seeing those opening day Dodger tickets begin to sprout wings and fly off into the distance.

"I don't have any evidence," I countered. Hunches are not evidence, although it was admittedly a gray area.

"All right. But I assume you're going to be continuing whatever it is you do. And if you uncover something, you better share it with us and I mean quick."

"Fair enough," I said.

"So who was the muckety-muck over at BMB that hired you? You recall that?"

"Name's Nick Roche. He's President of something or other there," I said and wrote down his phone number on the back of one of my business cards.

Juan took the card, looked at it and handed it to Roberto. "Give him a call tomorrow. Maybe even pay him a visit. Let's start putting a list together of people who might want to run over a former LAPD Lieutenant."

Roberto agreed and pocketed the card. Juan walked off to speak with the other investigators while Roberto waited until he was out of earshot. I shrugged at him.

"Sorry about that," I said. "I'll make sure you get your Dodger tickets, although I might have to slip them to you very surreptitiously."

"Do what you gotta do," he said. "I'm just hoping you'll still be walking around by then."

I peered at him. "You think I had something to do with this mess?"

"This?" Roberto said, pointing to the sheet that was still strewn haphazardly over the body. "No. But I picked up something from the Irvine P.D. this afternoon. They issued a warrant for your arrest."

I looked at him. "You've got to be kidding."

"I wish I were. Brandishing a weapon. Did you really threaten to shoot some rent-a-cop down in Orange County?"

Five

I was up early the next morning and so was Marcus. We watched a Baby Mozart DVD together, after which I offered him breakfast. He wanted waffles, and I convinced him Cheerios were the recommended choice on the menu today. If he agreed, I promised I'd take him to a magical place one night, where they served waffles for dinner. His eyes grew wide as he heartily agreed, and slowly went to work on his bowl of Cheerios. About half of the Cheerios went in his mouth, the other half wound up strewn on the floor.

Marcus actually was far more interested in my cup of French roast. I vaguely considered giving him a sip to provide a firsthand account of how strong black coffee really tasted. But then I recalled the time when Gail's parents came by to babysit one Saturday evening, so we could have a long overdue date night. Her parents gave him part of a can of Pepsi, and he was up well past midnight, wired in a manner we had never seen before. Marcus would undoubtedly hate the taste of coffee at this age, but I was a little more concerned about my wife's reaction to giving our toddler another dose of caffeine. I offered him a couple of red flame grapes instead, and he was marginally okay with that option.

My work day started at 7:30 a.m. After presiding over my son's power breakfast, I headed out for my own. Across the street from the Rancho Park Golf Course was the John O'Groats restaurant. Many years ago, this had started out as a small, family-owned coffee shop, but it had evolved into something akin to the BMB commissary. It was not unusual to see company executives, agents, and the occasional celebrity schmoozing over plates of blueberry pancakes.

I made it there on time, but my breakfast companion was a good 20 minutes late. Her arrival came in a form not dissimilar to a chaotic whirlwind. She simultaneously chatted on her phone, smiled at the hostess, and managed to wave to a few other patrons in the restaurant. She was able to juggle all of this deftly, even ordering a cup of coffee while finishing up her phone conversation, which ended precisely as she sat herself down across from me.

"Well, good morning, detective!" she exclaimed with a bright smile.

"Call me Burnside. It's easier."

"I can certainly do that. And I was so pleased to hear from you. And so soon! Do you have a script written already? If not, no biggie. I can hire a screenwriter to do that. Tell me some stories about cops and robbers!"

I laughed and took a sip of some coffee. It wasn't French roast, but it wasn't bad either. "I could tell you a few that would make your hair curl. Some of them even relate to me. But that's not why I called."

"Oh?" she said with a smile. "Well, now I'm really intrigued."

"Let me tamp your enthusiasm down a little," I said. "It sounds like you haven't heard about last night."

She shook her head and began talking a mile a

minute. "I had a late dinner with an actress who might or might not be right for this film we're casting. I don't know. She has a steep price tag, and we're already going over budget. But I had to fire someone yesterday, they just weren't getting along with the director. So I need to get a body and I mean quick. We started shooting last week and it's already a nightmare. You know how some pictures just seem jinxed?"

"No, but I'm not in the business."

"Oh well," she said. "I knew this would happen. Mercury went into retrograde last week. Never fails. Always a ton of screw-ups."

"And to think people believe making movies is fun."

"The fun part is in the beginning. Everything is possible. But yeah, the reality can be messy. Things move at breakneck speed. Too much stuff going on. It's a miracle some of these films even get done at all. And then last night my six year-old goes and wakes me up at 3:30 a.m., said she had a bad dream. Single parent, you can't imagine. My nightmares happen when I'm awake. I barely got her to school on time. I'm stretched a little thin. Oh. So what happened last night?"

"Hector Ferris was murdered," I said. I normally didn't deliver bad news this bluntly, but I needed to get her complete attention.

Patty Muckenthaler's jaw dropped and she blinked a few times. Maybe she was trying to wake up. A waiter poured a cup of coffee in front of her, but she didn't so much as look at it. The blank expression on her face told me she was trying very hard to comprehend what I just said.

"Who did it?" she finally asked.

"The police don't know yet," I answered, thinking this was an odd question. Nine times out of ten, people simply asked what happened. In her case, she wanted to hear the ending first. Maybe that was what a person did when they made movies.

"Oh, my," she said, still looking like she was in a daze. "I just saw him yesterday. He looked fine."

"Yes," I said, trying to figure her out. "Murder tends to happen suddenly."

Patty gazed down at her phone again and began scanning through news feeds frenetically. Some light touches of makeup graced her face, but not enough to hide the bags under her eyes. At a certain age, the many long nights catch up with us all.

"Here we go," she said excitedly. "But wait. It just says a former LAPD officer was run down. It doesn't say anything about BMB."

I looked at her. "The media. You know. They never get it straight," I said dryly.

"Isn't that the truth," she said, still working the phone. "Oh, okay. Yeah, I have a few texts about it. People asking if I heard about what happened. Something tragic."

"Right," I said as I studied her carefully. The idea that a senior executive would be unaware that her company's Security Director had been killed more than 12 hours ago was implausible. Yet here she was, putting on an act. And it was a good act. Nothing in her face or voice or mannerisms gave her away.

A waitress came over to take our order. I told her we weren't ready yet, but Patty broke in and waved a dismissive hand. Without bothering to look at a menu or even look up from her phone, she ordered a bowl of oatmeal with brown sugar. I shrugged and ordered some applewood smoked bacon, eggs over medium and buttermilk biscuits.

"How well did you know Hector?" I asked.

"Not well. But no one at BMB knew Hector well. Nick, maybe. But I think Hector wanted it that way. You know, every company has a Hector. He's there to protect the organization. Just like HR. Employees think Human Resources is there to help them, but they're not. They're there to minimize the company's risk."

"Can you tell me why you were meeting with Hector the other day?"

She paused for a moment, seemingly wondering how much she should reveal. "It's complicated. And I'm not sure it concerns you."

"Maybe not," I said. "Look, I was brought in to do background work on a CEO candidate. Hector was looking into him as well. I don't know if that had anything to do with Hector's murder. But the timing is curious. I'm just checking out all the possibilities."

Patty's mouth curled slightly when I mentioned the CEO search. She impatiently waited until I finished before responding. "A CEO candidate? You don't mean Eric Starr?"

"You know him?"

"Of course. Or his reputation anyway. He'd be a

disaster. Trust me. He doesn't understand our business."

"Is there something you can share?" I asked.

"Oh. Well. He has a bad rep when it comes to working with women," she managed, in a less-than-confident voice. "And that's one issue our company certainly doesn't need."

"No company needs that. But I keep hearing BMB and sexual harassment thrown around together. Why is that?"

Patty stared into her coffee for a minute. "A lot of it has to do with the industry," she finally said. "Entertainment is full of wounded people. Not all of the charges you hear about are legitimate. Some of them are trumped up. Hector was good at figuring out what was real."

"Whatever you know might help."

She raised the cup to her lips and blew softly into the coffee. "Listen, I manage a lot of people. Every time one of them files a complaint, I hear about it. And no, I can't share any details. There are confidentiality issues."

I began to get impatient. "Is that because you were one of the people Hector was investigating?"

She glared at me and slammed her cup down onto the saucer. Some coffee sloshed onto the tablecloth. Diners at surrounding tables looked over at us. "That's outrageous! What are you talking about?"

"I have reason to believe Hector was investigating you."

"And how would you know that?!" she demanded.

"Because he told me."

The slight curl of anger had now turned into an ugly

scowl. "I don't know what he told you," she said and suddenly got up to leave. "But I suspect whatever it was he was investigating, it died along with Hector."

*

The morning commute into downtown L.A. is an endless line of slow-moving vehicles trudging forward at a snail's pace. Traffic normally bottled up early, and didn't bust loose until after 10:00 a.m. For the last three years I had made this drive down to USC most mornings, but I usually left at the crack of dawn, so the Santa Monica Freeway was a breeze. When traffic was light, navigating L.A. was almost a pleasure. But except for long holiday weekends, when the city empties out and residents flee to more tranquil locales, good traffic days were rare. And today I didn't have much choice. My appointment was for 9:30 a.m., and I was told I was lucky to get it.

I still had my faculty parking pass, so I cruised easily onto the SC campus, although I didn't take one of the coaches' reserved spaces. Instead, I entered the parking structure next to the Dental School, off of Vermont and Jefferson, and wound my way up five levels before finding a space big enough to fit my SUV. I skipped quickly down the steps, passing a number of sleep-deprived students. Spring Break was a week away, and it looked like many of the kids needed the time off.

The USC School of Cinematic Arts was located right next to the sprawling John McKay Center, where I had spent much of the past three years. The McKay Center was the athletic complex that housed the training rooms, coaches' offices and an underground practice field. The student-athletes there were often big, muscular and cocky. The Cinema School, by contrast, had a far more eclectic crowd. From daydreaming future screenwriters to gorgeous aspiring actresses to some very weird people dressed in black, Cinema students were a stark contrast to the football players whom I had coached. But in the end, they were all just a group of focused young adults trying to navigate their way in the world. And unlike a lot of students, these kids not only had dreams of fame, but they often had plans mapped out to get there. Not all would make it, but at least they were trying.

The Cinema School occupied a series of seven connected buildings, with a small courtyard in the middle. Passing through an arched entryway, I pulled open a glass door with black iron trim and walked inside what some have called an architectural masterpiece. The University had spent the better part of a decade erecting new buildings, and this complex was the crown jewel. Atop one of the archways was a Latin inscription, *Limes Regiones Rerum* which translates to "Reality Ends Here."

It took me a few minutes to find Dr. Lucas Kanter's office. This journey was made longer by a number of misleading directives from students who appeared to be knowledgeable, but were, in fact, merely guessing. Good acting comes in many forms.

I rapped softly on the open door and a tall, slender, middle-aged man stood up and walked toward me. He had a distinguished appearance, thin, almost delicate features, and slicked-back brown hair. The dark green shirt looked expensive, as did the tailored slacks and tasseled loafers. He had a skeptical smile, but when he spoke he revealed a surprisingly deep, baritone voice that commanded presence.

"Coach Burnside," he said, his voice loaded with inflections. "I'm so pleased to finally meet you."

I smiled, mostly reflecting his enthusiasm. "And I, you."

"Please," he offered, motioning to a luxurious burgundy leather couch. I sat down and immediately sunk a few inches into the soft cushion. "I've met quite a few of the football staff, but I don't believe I ever had the pleasure of meeting you."

Lucas Kanter's office was plush for a professor, most faculty offices were largely utilitarian. His matching burgundy chair had a high back and chrome armrests, giving it a more regal look. His window faced a tranquil courtyard, and there were stacks of papers and files neatly piled on his oak desk. The book shelves were filled, floor-to-ceiling, with an array of books and scripts.

"I declined a lot of faculty meet-and-greets," I acknowledged. "I probably should have gone to a few. Or at least to one, anyway."

"We do like to get to know one another on campus. And football coaches have a celebrity status, as I'm sure you're aware."

"You know I've left the University."

"Yes, yes, that was big news around here when Johnny moved on. Disappointing. And it looks as if the new coach has brought in his own people. The jury's still out on him."

I shook my head. The season hadn't even started yet, and the new coach was being judged before a single game had been played. Such is the world of big-time college football. "Once he wins 10 or 11 games, and the team goes to the Rose Bowl, I'm sure he'll be accepted."

"Well, we do celebrate our winners here."

"And you're quite the celebrity yourself," I pointed out.

Dr. Kanter held out his hands. "What I do is largely maneuvering behind the scenes. My career took off when a few of my scripts were turned into features. But luck plays a big role. Some of the best screenplays ever written are still lingering on producers' shelves."

"You've done a little bit of everything," I observed. "Writing, acting, directing."

"More by necessity. I started out as an actor. Trained at Stella Adler. I landed a few good roles at first, but being a performer is a tough life. Unless you hit it big, an actor has to do an awful lot of auditions. The rejection takes its toll."

"And you turned to writing to assuage that problem."

Kanter laughed. "You've got a nice vocabulary. I'd love to have seen the reaction on a football player's face when you used a word like assuage. But no. I started writing based on a tip I once received. I was attending a party following the premiere of a movie in which I had a small role. I was the eighth lead, basically a nobody, and some producer approached me. Elderly man, old Hollywood type, even wore an ascot. He said it was a shame I didn't have leading-man looks. So I'd need to learn how to write screenplays, pen one with a starring role for myself, and then insist on directing it, too."

"Interesting advice."

"Yes. He disappeared right after that, I have no idea who he was. But I took his advice and wrote a script for myself. The only problem was that no studio would let me play the lead. BMB finally let me direct it. And I discovered I liked what came with directing. I had to learn every bit of the filmmaking process. From location scouting to camera angles to editing."

"You did all that?"

"I didn't do any of that. This is show business, remember. But I had to understand it in order to direct others. In the end, what I liked most was teaching. To a large extent, that's what a director does. Teach. Not unlike a football coach. You know who's good at what, and you try and prepare them to do the best job they can. If you're lucky, it all comes together."

"And if it doesn't quite come together, you become a professor?"

"Or, I suppose, a private eye."

I smiled. "*Touché*. You've done your homework, too."

"I have a curious mind," he said. "But I heard Nick Roche was bringing you on board to do some detective work. You know, I didn't plan on teaching, but I didn't plan on earning a Ph.D. in Cinema either. I liked it, began studying it in-depth and well, here I am. Teaching bright young minds how to make movies. Including one of your football players, I should add."

"Really. Who?"

"Demetrius Goffney. Bright young man, has a lot of ideas. And quite an, er, interesting background. Growing up in South L.A., impoverished childhood, parents not around much. How he avoided the gang life is a miracle."

"Sometimes the gangs leave athletes alone," I said. "They know they're special. It's a level of respect."

Demetrius was one of my safeties, a player we sometimes called a tweener. He wasn't quite fast enough to be a great cornerback, and he didn't tackle sure enough to be a safety. But he was agile and he was smart. Demetrius had a knack for winding up in the right place at the right time. In college football that was sometimes enough. The NFL had stricter requirements, though.

"Give him my regards," I said. "He's a good kid."

"You might run into him on your way out. I'm trying to get him an internship at BMB, he's been asking about it. In fact, I had to push him back today, to make room to see you."

"I appreciate it. That brings us to the reason for my visit. I'd like to know a bit more about BMB."

"Anything in particular?"

"Mostly learn about a few people. You heard about what happened to Hector Ferris?"

He nodded. "Very tragic. I didn't know him personally, but it sounded like a horrible thing."

"Do you know Patty Muckenthaler?" I asked.

Dr. Kanter took a deep breath. I wasn't sure how much he was going to share with me. But the good professor struck me as someone who liked to show off his knowledge.

"Patty's a unique talent. Very left brain-right brain. She has creative chops, but she's also very organized. She has to be. Heading up Production for a long list of features and TV shows is a big job."

"But?"

"Ah, yes. But. You know how a person's biggest strength can also be their biggest weakness?"

"In a way, yes."

"Patty's drive and ambition led her to the top levels of a multinational corporation. She'd do anything to get ahead. But she expects others will also. That includes bosses, colleagues and underlings. And it's where things can go off the rails."

"By chance, does sexual harassment play into all this?"

"There have been allegations made."

"About her or by her?"

Kanter chuckled. "Well, I think you may be on to something. The scuttlebutt around the company is that she screwed her way to the top, but that's not really fair. It's also sexist. She's good at her job."

"But there have been dalliances," I continued.

"A few. Maybe more than a few, I honestly wouldn't know. But it's a part of the industry. And some people use these affairs as leverage. It happens in business. More often in our business, though."

I thought back to something that was still bothering me. "When I was introduced to Hector, he was finishing a meeting with Patty. Any idea as to what they could have been talking about?"

Kanter shook his head. "Could have been anything. Might not have been related to her, Patty oversees a big organization. But I guess if you wanted to find out more about her, you should talk to Malcolm Taylor, he was our last CEO. He's the one who promoted Patty to where she is. She was his *protégé*."

"Think he'd be willing to talk to me?"

"I can make a call. Mal's just over in Century City."

"Near my office," I pointed out. "Appreciate it."

"I'll let him know. He still has a relationship with BMB."

"You've lost a few CEOs in the past couple of years. Sounds like a tough job."

"It is. I've known Mal forever. We've been friends since seventh grade. Harvard-Westlake. Well, it was called the Harvard School back in the day. That's actually how I wound up at BMB. Malcolm brought me in. Said it would be prestigious for BMB to have someone from academia on the board of directors. And that certainly wouldn't hurt my standing at the University."

"I would imagine. You have nicer office furniture than I had."

"Within a big university, every little bit helps," he laughed.

"But it sounds like you couldn't help your friend much. He only lasted what, a year?"

"It's a rough job, CEO. Tons of pressure. But he'll be fine."

"How's that?"

"Golden parachute. When a guy at that level gets cut loose, companies hand them a bundle of money to ease the fall. Getting another CEO job is tough, there just aren't a lot of them around. And most of those guys know they're not going to be around for too long. It's a 24/7 job these days. High burnout rate."

"So this Malcolm Taylor negotiated a good exit package?"

"Did it before he even took the job. Executives get their severance agreement written into the contract. They have an exit package before they even start the job."

"Planning for failure. It's no wonder they don't last long."

Kanter shrugged. I had an idea. "Let's get back to Hector for a moment," I said. "Tell me something."

"Yes?"

I leaned forward. "You're a storyteller. You know something about motivation. If this were a movie you were directing, who would have killed Hector Ferris?"

Kanter stiffened and gave me a hard-edged look. "This is real life, Mr. Burnside."

"It is. But it's not getting me very far."

"I thought you were brought in to look into Eric Starr's background. This is above and beyond your assignment, isn't it?"

"Sure. And maybe Hector's murder isn't related to Eric Starr. Most likely it's not. But what if it is?"

Lucas Kanter gave me a long look and glanced over at his computer monitor. It was as if he hadn't heard me. "It appears as if my next appointment is here. I'm glad you stopped by, Mr. Burnside. I'll call Malcolm. And let me know if you need anything else."

I didn't like being dismissed in this manner, but nor did I want to make an issue out of it. Nothing would be gained by pushing him now. I said a polite goodbye and walked out of his office. But as I started down the hall, I caught a glimpse of a familiar face. He didn't see me, but only because he was doing what young people are prone to do, walking while looking down at his iPhone. I moved into his path and cleared my throat, but he barely noticed, opting to walk around me instead of looking up. I tried another tact.

"Hey, number thirty," I barked, referring to the uniform number he wore on the field. "I guess you forgot the lesson I taught you about keeping your head on a swivel."

Demetrius Goffney jerked his head up in surprise and then broke into a wide grin. "Hey-hey, Coach!" he shouted and moved to give me a hug. "I didn't think I'd see you around here so soon. Or ever, maybe."

"I have a lot of ties to this place, Demetrius. It's like I said when I recruited you. Back when you were torn between whether to commit to UCLA or USC. You remember what I said?"

"Oh yeah," he giggled. "You're a Bruin for four years and a Trojan for life. I still hear it. It's like a mantra around this place."

"That's why we call it Trojan Family. So how're you doing with the new coaches?"

"Okay, I guess. This was supposed to be my breakout

year. I was looking to be a starter. Junior year, you know. Feels like I have to prove myself all over again."

"That's always going to be the case," I warned him. "Everywhere, and not just football. You're always being evaluated."

"I was hoping to start at safety. They have me back at cornerback. Second string."

"Things might work out," I told him. "But you can help yourself. Volunteer for special teams. Everyone needs a good gunner. And realistically, you might wind up being a nickel back. Coming in on third down passing situations. That might suit you. You're smart. And teams need smart players on third down."

He looked at me and processed this. "Okay. I hear you. Seems like you're still coaching me."

"Well, I hope you learned a few things."

"Yeah," he laughed. "I still remember when I was in high school. You told our coach to always have his players wear gloves the color of the opposing team's jerseys. Cuts down on holding calls."

"Uh, right," I said, my face feeling like it might be getting red. I pointed to Dr. Kanter's office. "What are you doing here? I didn't know you were a Film major."

Demetrius smiled. "I was majoring in NFL," he said, "but I finally started thinking about the stuff you and Coach Cleary were preaching all along. Make the most of your time here. Study something you like. Use the university, just like the university is using you. You never know what might happen. It didn't really sink in until you guys left."

Back in the day, I had also hoped to get a shot at the NFL. But my pro football ambitions were short-circuited due to a freak accident assisting a USC campus security officer. I helped him chase down a petty thief, but in so doing, tore the ACL in my knee. It happened in the spring of my senior year, and with the absence of today's medical advances, no NFL team would take a chance on drafting me. My knee healed, but not enough for me to chase down a speedy wide receiver. And thus, a career in law enforcement began.

"Funny how that all works," I said. "Your perspective changes when you start to look beyond college, at the real world."

"Yeah. I had taken a few film courses, but now I'm getting serious about it. And I wrote a script. That's what I'm here for this morning. I need someone to give me notes."

"What's the story about?

"Well, I got this idea. Off-duty cop sees a gang murder about to go down. He intervenes. But a couple of local guys jump him and take his gun. They hit him over the head, use his gun in the murder and then call 911. He wakes up next to a dead body and gets arrested. The cop gets charged for a crime he didn't commit."

I drew in a long breath and again thought back on my own history. My bad luck had nothing to do with a murder, but it was pretty serious. And there were parallels. Many years ago I befriended a teenage runaway being charged with prostitution. The type of situation in which a cop should never be involved. I let my guard down and got burned. I was falsely accused of running a prostitution ring, something that was ridiculous beyond my wildest dreams. The fallout led to my being arrested, and I was looking at serious jail time. While I was eventually exonerated, I was also a changed man. And a changed cop, which led to my getting discharged from the LAPD. It happened years ago, but it still felt fresh in my mind. And hearing Demetrius detail his story made it seem like it happened yesterday. I felt the hairs standing up on the back of my neck.

"So, Demetrius," I said, feeling a little apprehensive. "How does this story end?"

"Well, that's what I want to speak with Dr. Kanter about. I'm not sure how to get a happy ending out of this. It's not so easy if you want to make it believable. Right now the ending looks kind of bleak."

Six

Century City is not really a city. It's not even a neighborhood. Wedged between Beverly Hills and Westwood, it is technically a part of Los Angeles, a cluster of high-rise office towers, hotels, condos, and a glitzy outdoor shopping mall. It is a compact community, a freakishly oversized business park, one where few people actually live, but where many go to both earn and spend their lofty paychecks. While Century City measures only about eight or nine blocks, they are a very valuable eight or nine blocks indeed.

Malcolm Taylor's offices were in the gleaming Century Plaza Towers, a pair of silver, triangular-shaped structures that serve as a guidepost for any tourist or newbie trying to navigate through the Westside. The towers had been around for more than four decades, each one rising 44 stories, chrome pyramids that employed vertical black and gray lines to make them appear even more imposing than they already were. Over the years, other skyscrapers were erected in the L.A. basin, but outside of downtown, Century City still had the two tallest buildings in southern California.

I rode the quiet elevator up to the 38th floor and entered an even quieter hallway, cloaked in a hushed coolness. At the end of the corridor was a door with "Celestial Productions" in gleaming gold letters on the nameplate. I walked in and came upon a well-built, handsome middle-aged man, hunched over a desk, combing haphazardly through some documents. He was looking intently for something, and either didn't notice that I had walked in or simply didn't care. He wore what looked like an expensive black shirt, open at the throat, and dressy black slacks. On his right wrist was a thick gold braided bracelet, on his left was a watch with a distinctive silver-and-gold band. I cleared my throat. He still didn't look up, but at least he acknowledged my presence.

"You can just leave your script over there," he said in a smooth voice that sounded as if it had been the product of many years of training. The voice sounded like one I had heard before on the radio. Or maybe on a game show. "We'll get back to you."

"I'm not peddling a script," I said.

"Then what do you want?"

"I'm here to see Malcolm Taylor."

The man looked up. A closer look revealed he was indeed very handsome, the type of handsome that some people might even swoon over. His blond hair was very blond and his blue eyes were bright and sparkling. He had the type of look you sometimes saw in actors, the kind who always managed to get work.

"Sorry. He's gone to a lunch meeting," the very good-looking man said. "Don't know when he'll be back."

"That's strange," I said. "I had an appointment. Lucas Kanter at USC set it up."

He looked up at me again. "You're Burnside."

"I am indeed."

"Why didn't you say so? I'm not a mind reader."

"You're Taylor?"

"Of course I am," he said, offended that I hadn't recognized him.

"Sorry," I smiled. "How stupid of me. I just didn't think a former CEO would drop such a casual lie."

He shook his head. "What business are you in?"

"Let's just say I'm transitioning."

"Uh-huh," he said, nodding in a condescending way. "Well, if you want to make it in this business, you've got to know who the players are. You've got some work ahead of you."

"I suppose. That assumes I want to be in this business."

"Everyone wants to be in this business."

"Sure. Look, I'd like a few minutes of your time. I have a few questions. Confidential. Did Dr. Kanter tell you anything more than I'd be coming to see you?"

"No, Lucas just left a message," he sighed. "I thought it would be one of his students dropping off a script. All right, look, I've got a minute. Come on in."

I followed him into what might be called a suite, a vast amount of space that could have easily been transformed into a bowling alley. The huge oak desk was set near the windows, with a sitting area nearby that held a couch and a few easy chairs. On the other side of the room were several tables, a few of which were piled high with scripts. Off in a corner was an 80-inch TV, mounted on a wall, with just one chair facing it.

"So I figured you'd have an assistant," I said, handing Malcolm Taylor my business card and taking a seat across from his desk. He moved slowly around it, perusing a few papers before sitting down onto what more aptly resembled a throne rather than a desk chair.

Taylor took off his watch, clearly a Rolex. He placed it face up on the desk, a trick I had seen before. This was a power move, the type of signal that communicates that this man's time is valuable. And time with him will be limited. When the watch is placed face down, it means the opposite; the visitor's presence is valued and they can take all the time they'd like.

"Of course I have an assistant," he sniffed. "Adam wanted to come in late today. The slug. He thinks just because he worked until midnight last night he can slough off."

"Imagine that," I said.

"Ah, he's not a bad kid. Been with me since I ran Production over at BMB."

"BMB. That's why I'm here."

"Of course that's why you're here. Once the trades announced I was leaving BMB with a three-picture deal as part of my package, I've had everyone in town pay me a visit. Even some people I actually know."

I put up my hands. "Relax," I said wearily. "Again. I'm not in the industry. I'm not looking to sell you anything."

Taylor sat back and looked at me like I was from another planet. "Well, that's a first. I can't even imagine what you want then."

"Uh, yeah. Well, it's a little delicate. I'm a Private Investigator. I started out by doing a background investigation for BMB. But after what happened last night, my work has expanded."

"What happened last night?"

"Hector Ferris?" I asked, wondering if these folks read anything beyond *The Hollywood Reporter.* "Did you hear?"

He nodded grimly. "Yes, sorry. Awful thing. A real blow. But I've moved past BMB. My time there is finished and I'm starting a new chapter."

"Okay. Did you know Hector well?"

"No, not really. Didn't interact much with him. I had bigger things on my plate."

"How about Patty Muckenthaler?"

"Patty? Of course I knew Patty. I made her head of Production when I took over. Wait a minute. You think Patty had something to do with Hector?"

"Do you?" I asked, answering a question with a question.

Malcolm Taylor considered this as he glanced out of his of east-facing window. It was turning into another clear day, and you could almost see into the San Gabriel Valley. The Library Tower capped the downtown skyline, its glass crown having made it another very recognizable landmark in L.A. The official name of the building had changed some years ago, but many Angelenos kept calling it the Library Tower rather than dignifying the soulless corporation that purchased it, and renamed the structure after itself.

"That's an interesting question," he mused. "At first thought, no, who would ever think Patty capable of doing such a gruesome thing. No matter what the benefit to her."

"Benefit?"

"Oh, well, I may have been speaking out of turn. Patty's an ambitious woman. Hector was probably looking into a harassment case, that was much of what his job required. I heard this one involved a woman who reported up to Patty. It was mostly nonsense, but some people take these things seriously."

"I thought you'd moved on from BMB. New chapter and all," I said.

"I stay in touch with some people. You have to in this business. It's all about relationships."

"So who was the woman?"

Malcolm Taylor smiled. It was the type of smile that was broad and powerful. "I'm not at liberty to say. Confidentiality and all."

"That's going to be a tough line to maintain when the police start grilling you. And I assume they'll find out anyway when they look into Hector's records. You can save some time by talking to me."

"Now listen," he said, his voice growing a little stern. "Patty's a colleague, we may work together in the future. As I've said, relationships in the industry are critical. I'm not going to be a party to getting her into any more trouble than she's already in."

"Funny thing," I observed. "Everyone knows a little something here, a little something there. Yet no one wants to actually say anything."

Malcolm Taylor held up his hands. "It's like a movie that's been put in turnaround. Everyone wants to distance themselves from the stench. If you knew the business, you'd understand."

"You guys have a strange way of talking." I shook my head. "And to think people complain about that with me."

"How long have you been a detective?" he asked, giving me an odd look, almost like a museum-goer trying to make sense of an abstract painting.

"Private Investigator. I had my own agency for years after leaving the LAPD. Took a break to coach football at SC. Now I'm back."

"How long were you part of the LAPD?"

"A long time. Why?"

"I could maybe use someone like you," he said, thinking this through. "Technical advisor. Got a crime picture I'm developing, I need someone to make sure the police procedural stuff is accurate. Pays well. You interested?"

I looked at him. After what I'd seen over the past few days, I didn't have the slightest interest in working in show business. But this investigation wasn't moving forward at the speed I wanted. And I didn't like saying no to anything right away. After my football career ended, my old coach, Bulldog Martin, made the comment that no one should ever dismiss an opportunity without considering it. And the older you get, he said, the less frequently opportunities come along.

"How does maybe sound?"

"I'll take that as a yes," he said presumptuously. "Adam will call you later. He'll have an agreement drawn up."

I shrugged and said okay. That is, okay to reviewing the agreement. Signing it would be another story, something I'd need to think about. A business relationship was like any other relationship. Pick the right partner and it's great. Pick the wrong partner and you may have a lamp thrown at you at some point. My initial thought was it might be best to wait until my current case was put to bed. Especially since I was hired to investigate Taylor's potential successor, something I'd need to reveal to him sooner if not later. I finally decided there was no time like the present.

"There's something else I need to ask you about," I said.

"Oh?" he asked, looking down at his Rolex as if to signal my time was nearly up.

"This is a little delicate, too."

"What, is everything delicate with you? Come on. I've seen blood spattered all over a movie set. Not much is going to shock me these days."

"All right," I said, starting to feel the need to rub the bridge of my nose. "I'm looking into Eric Starr. Anything you know about him? Anything you can share?"

Malcolm Taylor looked at me like I had just vomited on his rug. "Eric Starr?! Yeah, I know him. I heard someone on the board wants to replace me with that retard. Guy knows nothing about the business, he's an Internet jock. But some people at BMB think that worm can just slide in and run the show."

"Why do you say that? He built Laputa out of nothing."

"Take a good look at Laputa and you'll see it's still nothing. It's falling apart. Half the people who work there hate his guts, the other half are scared to death of him. He murdered his partner. Or had him murdered, I guess."

I blinked a few times. "You sound rather sure of that."

"That was the rumor around town," he said and then began to backpedal. "Aw, look, the board can do whatever they like at this point. I don't care. I have an iron-clad contract to do three pictures with BMB. Might even be good medicine for them if Starr took over. Maybe they'd see I didn't do such a bad job."

"Sounds like you've thought about it."

"Of course I've thought about it," he said as he stood up. "What do you imagine I do all day? I think about things. And look, I don't mean to cut this short, but I actually do have an early lunch meeting I need to get to. As I said, Adam will follow up on our agreement. You'll like the money."

Walking out of Malcolm Taylor's office took a surprising number of steps. Why anyone needed an office that was large enough to hold a touch football game was beyond me. An office fit for a king. Or maybe someone who liked to believe he was.

As I moved into the reception area, I came upon a young man talking fast into a phone. He was smartly dressed in a blue shirt and tie. He also wore a watch with a silver-and-gold band, one that looked like a Rolex. On Malcolm Taylor it looked natural. On this young man, it did not.

"Yeah, we need it now," he barked into the phone.

"Five minutes? I guess. Mr. Taylor's leaving soon. Okay. Sure. No. Not ten minutes. Five. Four would be better. Thanks. Bye."

He hung up and looked at me.

"You must be Adam," I said.

"I must be. Adam Gee. Who are you?"

"Name's Burnside. I may be doing some work for Malcolm."

"All right. What kind of work?"

"Technical advisor. He said something about making a crime picture."

"Hmmm. Maybe that's *Day Shift*. Or *Day Watch*. We have a few in development."

"I wouldn't know. He didn't say."

"All right. I'll check with him and get back to you. May I have your contact info?"

I handed him a business card. "Tough night last night?"

"Excuse me?" he asked, looking up at me with a quizzical expression.

"Nothing," I said. "Just something your boss mentioned. You working late and all."

"Oh yeah. Comes with the territory. We had an industry function. This AFI reception."

"Must be fun to work here. Nice opportunity working with a high-level guy."

"Yes. It's great to have a mentor like Malcolm."

I sometimes wondered what my life would have been like if I had a mentor guiding my journey after I had graduated from college. Bulldog Martin had been my surrogate father at SC, but there was only so much career guidance he could provide beyond football. I had to figure everything out on my own. While it was satisfying to look back and see the life I had carved out, the path that led me here was a circuitous one. And rocky at times. Sometimes a helping hand pays off, but it was a luxury I could only imagine.

"That's a nice watch," I said. "You must be doing okay."

He held up his wrist. "This thing? It was a Christmas present last year from BMB. Everyone at the company got one. Looks like a Rolex, but it said BMB on the face initially. A lot of us around the company went and had new faceplates put in that just said Rolex. You can fool a lot of people that way. Kind of an inside joke."

*

After grabbing a quick lunch at the food court of the crowded Century City mall, I drove slowly back to my office. This was my third day of working for BMB and Nick Roche. I had uncovered quite a bit, but not what I was actually hired to uncover. I called Roberto De Santos, and while the police were still chasing down leads on the Hector Ferris homicide, no obvious suspects were on their radar. I told him about my morning. Aside from Patty Muckenthaler being stunningly unaware that a colleague had been murdered, nothing else jumped out as suspicious. But as I drove past Westwood, an idea popped into my head.

Parking at UCLA is always a challenge, especially for someone who enters that hilly campus infrequently and doesn't know the terrain. I finally found a space in a garage near Pauley Pavilion and was grateful I hadn't put any USC license plate holders on my new Pathfinder. Getting key scratches removed was a bother. After entering the Morgan Athletic Center, I found some interns but none of them could tell me anything about Coach Strong's whereabouts. Maybe they were trained to be obsequious, guiding an unknown visitor back out of the building, assuming he didn't belong there. Fortunately, one of the football program's assistant coaches recognized me.

"Oh, you think this is an open house, Burnside," called a grinning, oversized man wearing a blue t-shirt with the word PERSEVERANCE in big gold letters.

"Hey there, big fella," I smiled in return. Big fella usually works when addressing a coach, especially since I never bothered to learn opposing coaches' names. Networking in the coaching community was not a strong suit for me. In some ways, I always sensed my coaching career would be short-lived.

"You planning to steal some plays from us?" he grinned.

"Nah," I said, wondering if I should remind him USC had won five of the last six games between our cross-town rivals. "Not necessary. Just looking for Jay."

"Oh yeah, your Trojan buddy. He's over in the gym pumping iron. Guy goes non-stop. Glad we took him off your hands."

I shrugged. "Not my decision. New coach, new regime. You know, I'm not there any longer, either."

"Tough luck. You'll find something. We're all nomads in this business. Speak well of others and carry a warm resume, that's my philosophy."

After a few more minutes of mindless chatter, he directed me to the weight room. It was largely empty, with most players in class during this time of the day. As a result, the sound of one man's deep and agonizing grunting reverberated throughout the room, as Jay Strong did ten bench presses, repeatedly jerking up a barbell loaded with free weights. By my estimate, it held over 300 pounds. A muscle-bound spotter stood close by in case Jay needed any help, but that proved unnecessary. Jay returned the bar carefully to its place, got up, and wiped some residual sweat off the padded bench he had been lying on.

"Haven't lost your touch," I commented.

"Hey, Burnside!" he exclaimed. "Twice in one week. I feel honored."

I turned to the spotter, who had the same body type as Jay, wide and solid, although he looked 15 years younger. He was brimming with an eager-to-please expression pasted on his face, and he looked like a graduate assistant who aspired to be a coach himself one day.

"Say, pal," I turned to him. "Can you give us a few minutes?"

The spotter looked hesitantly at Jay, who shrugged and pointed to the locker room. "I can take it from here, Sean."

I waited until Sean had departed. Now it was just the two of us in the weight room. "I'm looking more into BMB and finding some funny things. Issues of sexual harassment. Lot of turnover at the top. And then their head of Security got killed yesterday."

Jay looked away. "I heard. Like I told you the other day. It's a crazy place."

"I know your wife works there," I said, watching him carefully. "I'm wondering if Kitty's said anything to you. Anything you can share."

Jay mopped his face with the same towel he had used to wipe off the bench. He looked at the towel and then tossed it on the ground. He didn't reply, but it was clear he was thinking about something.

"Sounds like you might have some inside knowledge," I prodded.

"It's not a good situation," he finally muttered.

"Jay. I don't want to pry here," I said, trying to be as delicate as possible. "Something's eating at you. Talking about it might help."

"Yeah, sure," he said absently.

I decided to take a shot. Revealing you have personal information about a person can sometimes unleash things, hopefully not a punch in the nose.

"Look, I still have friends on the job. I know the police have been to your home a few times. Domestic disturbances. I'm not going to tell anyone. And I wouldn't blame you if you told me to go take a hike. But I was a police officer for 13 years. And I've seen these scenarios play out. Whenever the police get repeatedly called to a residence, something is likely to happen, and it's usually something bad."

He looked at me. "You know about the police visits?"

"Yes."

Jay Strong took a deep breath and then exhaled loudly. "I swear, all of our problems started when we moved out here. We were married for 10 years back in Mississippi and never had an issue. We were happy together. Then we come out to L.A., Kitty takes this job, and everything changes."

"How'd all this happen?"

"I don't know," he sighed. "It's different out here. A lot of temptation. No morals. No limits. People thinking they can do anything. Get away with anything. And the money, man, the money. It's unreal."

"What do you mean?"

"It's like, I make a good living, right? You know that. Well into six figures. Back home that made me one of the top dogs. Out here, that doesn't even put me in the game. Do you know we couldn't even afford to buy a house in our neighborhood? We got turned down for a mortgage."

"Jay, you live in Brentwood," I pointed out. "It's very pricey real estate."

"Kitty tells people at BMB that we rent an apartment. They look at her like she's on welfare. She drives a brand new Toyota, but everyone she works with wonder why she isn't driving something better. People out here get their self-esteem from what they own."

"Okay," I said. Not a lot of this was new, but one thing was puzzling. "Didn't she grow up in Mississippi, like you?

I assume she'd have the same values."

Jay raised his palms in resignation. "I thought so, too. But her sister... " he said, his voice trailing off.

"What about her sister?" I peered at him. "Nick Roche's wife?"

"Yeah. Her sister puts on airs. Makes Kitty feel like she's missing out. Her sister went and married some guy making a fortune and spending it freely. She and Nick spent last Christmas skiing in the Swiss Alps. Kitty spent hers alone, I was prepping for the Rose Bowl."

"I remember the hours we put in," I said. "So what does she want from you? More time or more money? If you become a head coach one day, you'd be doing amazingly well. And frankly, I think you're doing pretty well right now," I said, reminding myself that one person's ceiling is another person's floor.

"Kitty's got stars in her eyes," he said. "And I think she's having an affair."

I took a breath. Things were becoming a little clearer. "Has she admitted it?"

"No, she won't do that. Deny, deny, deny, that's the tune she keeps playing. But Kitty has a lot of late nights. And business trips. I don't know with who yet, but I'm going to find out. It's been going on for a while. I'm tired of it. Sick and tired of it."

I took this in but needed to remind him of something. "You know, Jay. You weren't exactly faithful yourself."

He spun around and his eyes met mine. He glared at me in a challenging way. "How would you know that?"

"Because I've been on recruiting trips with you," I

Benjamin Starr was a short, stubby man with a wide face and a big nose. He had jet black hair that looked like it had recently been colored, not a silver thread was visible. He walked with purpose and strode right up to us. He didn't look very happy.

"Mrs. Walsh," he nodded and then turned angrily to me. "Sir, may I ask what you think you're doing?"

"You can ask, but I don't have to tell you."

Starr looked like I had slapped him in the face with a fish. Obviously he wasn't used to being treated in a way that wasn't deferential.

"You have a lot of nerve going around this street, poking into my family's business."

"How do you know what I'm doing?" I asked. "Mrs. Walsh and I are just talking about the Anteaters."

"The what?"

"Anteaters," I repeated. "That's the nickname for UC-Irvine. Their basketball team's having a good year, they even made it into the NCAA tournament. I'm surprised you didn't know that, you being such a big supporter of the local college and all."

"I have better things to do. Now why don't you get the hell out of here."

"Why don't you try to make me."

Benjamin Starr stared at me incomprehensibly, then reached into his pocket, turned his back to me and began fiddling with his phone. He looked back one more time to offer a nasty glare, and then walked over to the sidewalk.

"Touchy fellow," I said. And then, not more than 30 seconds later, we heard the screeching of tires coming reminded him. There had been a few instances where, late at night, I had seen Jay working a girl at the hotel bar. And a few times when a companion would come out of Jay's room in the morning.

"And tell me something," he demanded. "You never dipped into the honey pot?"

"Would it shock you if I said no?"

I was married to a beautiful woman, and the same temptations also presented themselves to me. But I also knew I couldn't pursue them. It had taken me too long to meet the girl of my dreams. And now with Marcus, I owed both of them some self-restraint.

Jay took a breath and looked down again. "We haven't had a perfect marriage. But I never talked about leaving Kitty. And I never did anything here in town that could get back to her. I'm not saying what I did was right. But I never rubbed her face in it."

My mouth tightened. "I'm sorry, Jay. But these things can be patched up. If that's what you want."

"Oh, yeah," he said. "Man, I don't want to lose her."

I thought of telling him that forgiveness and being open were good first steps toward any reconciliation. But admitting infidelity complicates matters to an extraordinary degree. Some things can be just too hard to forgive.

"You try a marriage counselor?" I asked.

"Kitty was pushing for it awhile ago. Then she stopped. I don't know. Maybe she's given up. Maybe this is her way of starting to separate. But it's tearing me up inside."

"You're not the first person to go through this," I said. "Ask her again about counseling. You never know. And even if she says no, maybe you should try to see someone on your own."

"Me? By myself?"

"Sure. Can't hurt."

Jay let out a low whistle. "You L.A. guys. Into all that touchy-feely stuff."

I laughed. "I'm hardly a poster boy for sensitive male behavior," I said, knowing we are all better at giving advice than taking it. But in this area, I did feel like I had some expertise. I had a good marriage and was committed to having it stay that way. Even living in a place like L.A.

Seven

I checked my cell phone right after leaving Jay. I had felt the distracting buzz of an incoming call, but wasn't about to interrupt my conversation with him. The call turned out to be from a blocked number, but the woman leaving the voice mail was very specific. Eric Starr wanted to see me this afternoon at 4:00 pm sharp. At his office.

The Laputa Complex was on Olympic Boulevard. in West L.A., along a parkway near the Santa Monica border. Driving along, you would have no idea it was close to Santa Monica or whether you had actually moved into a different city. There were no markers, no welcome billboards; in fact, the only discernible difference were the street signs. In Santa Monica, they had a cute yellow sun shining over the street names.

I arrived at Laputa at a little after 3:00 p.m. and parked in the subterranean garage. It was actually quite a nice garage, with rows wide enough for two cars to easily drive through. I knew this because an SUV barreling towards me from the other direction, barely slowed down to make room. The parking spaces were also large, and the special section for compact cars was well marked. Unlike some parking garages, seemingly constructed with the goal of cramming in as many vehicles as possible, the architect of this one actually gave consideration to the drivers before building it.

With an hour to kill, I walked down a sunny street for

an iced coffee at the local Starbucks. Unlike those in a typical strip mall, this Starbucks was housed on the first floor of a five-story office building. Next to it was the usual sandwich chain, dry cleaners, and the ubiquitous 7-Eleven. Structures like this had been sprouting up all over the Westside for the past few years, catering to Internet startups in what was now being referred to as Silicon Beach. I'm sure these companies added a windfall to the local economy. I knew for a fact they also added a lot of vehicles to the snarled local traffic. Come 4:00 pm, the eastbound streets heading out of West L.A. were gridlocked with teeth-gnashing motorists. Growth often comes with an unforeseen price tag, usually paid for by people other than the ones who profit from it.

I sat at a small table next to two young women, both of whom had Laputa badges clipped to their jeans. I listened to their conversation, hoping for a juicy morsel about work, but they were only chatting about their unreliable boyfriends. I added two packets of sugar to my icy drink, stirred hard, and took a long, pleasurable sip. I liked the flavor, both bitter and sweet at the same time. I began to feel good again. The miracle drug, caffeine, was kicking in, relaxing and energizing me at the same time. I looked at the young women and tried to conjure up an opening line that a middle-aged man in his 40s could utter to a pair of 20-somethings without sounding creepy. None came to mind, so when their conversation hit a lull, I jumped in with two left feet.

"So ... you both work for Laputa?" I asked stupidly.

"Uh, yeah," one of them replied, tying her brown hair

back into a small ponytail.

"Must be a cool place to work."

"I guess. The pay's not great, but we get free snacks," said the other one, a pretty strawberry blonde, as she started to giggle.

"Well, that's something. What do you do there?"

"We both work in UX," said the blonde.

"UX?" I asked.

"User Experience. We test out upgrades and new releases of the apps before they go live. We bring in people and ask them to try and complete tasks. We measure how long it takes them, and whether they're confused."

"Sounds like important work."

The girl with the brown ponytail rolled her eyes. The name on her badge was Olivia. "It ought to be. But our insights never quite make it to the top. Even if they do, they get watered down. Or the higher-ups put in temporary fixes that just make things worse."

"Must be frustrating," I said. "On the outside, people think Laputa is well run. I guess you never know."

"Yeah. I thought so, too. Before I started working there. Now I wonder if the Company will even be around in five years."

The blonde gave her a gimlet-eyed look, as if to tell her she was talking too much. Olivia stopped for a moment before shrugging at her friend. "Who cares. Feels like everyone in the world knows what's going on."

I watched them for a moment and decided to push forward with something else. "So do you ever see Eric Starr?"

They both started to squirm at the same time. "Once or twice," the blonde said. "Mostly glad we don't."

"Oh?' I said, trying to sound interested without sounding too interested.

"Eric has been known for, uh, dating within the office," Olivia said, sneaking a glance around the room to see if anyone else might be in earshot. "But they're all that way. Executives. It's like that for guys at the top."

I nodded. "Did that include Eric's old partner?

"Jack?" she clarified.

"Yeah."

"Sure. In fact, a woman I worked with once dated Jack Beale. Before the accident, obviously."

My ears perked up. "Is this woman still at Laputa?"

"No," she replied. "I guess Wanda was pretty broken up over what happened. She moved back to Australia."

"That's too bad," I said. "Say, wasn't Jack married?"

"Sure. But that never stops guys at that level. It's better to not be on their radar. Especially Eric's."

"Really?"

"Yeah, girls who go out with him don't last long with the company. He gets bored and next thing you know, they're gone." Olivia said, snapping her fingers. "Why are you interested in all this?"

I shrugged. "Just making conversation. Eric's a celebrity. I guess you know that."

They agreed, albeit cautiously, and then hastily excused themselves. I gave them a few minutes so they could reach Laputa and not see me as I started walking back there myself. It was 3:50 p.m. when I entered the lobby, which had, in large green letters, the LAPUTA logo plastered high up on one wall. I approached a pretty, doe-eyed receptionist who looked like she was in her early 20s.

"Hello there," I started.

"Hello," she beamed. "How can I help you?"

"I have a 4:00 p.m. with Eric Starr. My name's Burnside. I'm a few minutes early."

She looked over at a computer monitor. Her eager smile disappeared, and a frown emerged on her face. "Oh," she said. "Let me call upstairs."

The receptionist punched a few buttons on her phone and talked briefly into it before hanging up. "Why don't you have a seat for a minute. Someone's checking on this."

I sat down. About ten minutes later, the elevator dinged and another woman in her 20s emerged and approached me. She was also young and pretty. Everyone at Laputa was young and pretty.

"Hi, I understand you're here to see Eric."

"I am."

"I don't have you down on my calendar. Did Eric set this up with you on his own? He does that sometimes."

"No. In fact, I just got a call this afternoon, asking that I come over to meet with him."

"Do you know what this was regarding?"

I began to think that sharing any more information would not be helpful. "Sorry, no. Any idea of who might have set this up?"

"Not really. I'm his assistant and I keep his calendar. He's been in meetings all day. I can find out more if you'd like and call you."

"Sure," I said and handed her a business card. I thought of something. "Do you by any chance use a blocked number when you call someone?"

"I personally don't. But some of the executives do. Eric does sometimes. Depends on whether he wants the call to be a surprise."

I thanked her and walked slowly back to the elevator. This waste of time resembled a practical joke without the punch line, the sort of sophomoric locker-room prank that football players might pull on someone. But it just didn't add up. That is, until I got off the elevator and started toward my Pathfinder. The garage was warm and oddly quiet. Then suddenly, everything began to crystallize.

A pair of men came out of nowhere and stepped in front of me. One was burly, wearing jeans and a tight black t-shirt that showed off his large biceps. The other was gangly, wearing khakis, a cheap golf shirt and a gray hoodie. I stopped and looked at them.

"Burnside. We need to talk," the gangly one declared, motioning to a maroon van parked nearby.

"We don't need to do anything," I countered, wondering how he knew my name. "Except for you to get out of my way."

"Come on. I'm not asking. I'm telling you."

I looked around the empty garage. The air felt stark and motionless. I looked back at the two of them. "It's a little early for April Fools'," I said.

"You calling us fools?" said the gangly one in a challenging voice. "You should watch your mouth."

I looked at them. "With whom do I have the pleasure

of speaking?"

"Get in the van and we'll talk," he said, motioning again to the maroon vehicle a few yards away.

"We'll talk here," I said.

The two glanced at each other and the gangly one gave a knowing nod. He reached back and pulled a black snub-nose handgun out of the pocket of his hoodie. Pointing it at my abdomen, he gestured silently to the van with his gun.

Once you step into a vehicle at gunpoint, there is a very good chance you will not come out alive. And if you do, it might only be to dig your own grave. The odds of emerging unscathed from this type of situation are slim. The odds are actually better to make a run for it, zig-zagging to prevent a clear shot, and hope that the gunman has poor aim. But the garage was unfamiliar. And without knowing where the stairway was, a clean getaway would be difficult. The other option was to engage them directly. This offered me the best chance for survival. It also offered me the best chance of getting killed on the spot.

"Let's move," the gangly man said.

"Which way?" I asked.

The burly man pointed to the van. I raised my hands high over my head and began walking very slowly.

"Put your damn hands down!" the gunman ordered.

I stopped and turned to him, keeping my hands in the air. This was one way to get attention in case anyone else entered the garage. It was also a lot easier to attack with a downward motion. But it seemed as if my new friends might be aware of this trick. They kept their distance, a few yards away.

"Sorry," I said. "I thought this was supposed to be a stickup."

"It's not a stickup, you idiot. Just walk to the van."

"Well, if it's not a stickup, then what is it?" I demanded. "I'm just trying to follow the rules here."

"Hey, damn it, put your hands down. And I mean now."

I lowered my hands to shoulder height. "Well, I wish you'd make up your mind. If it's not a stickup, then what do you want?"

The gangly man rolled his eyes in exasperation. As if on cue, the burly man took a few steps forward and grabbed my left elbow with his right hand. Which was exactly what I'd hoped he'd do. Slamming my fist deep into his abdomen, he grunted as I grabbed his right arm, ducked underneath it and twisted it behind his back in one motion. I applied sharp pressure to his wrist and yanked his arm halfway up his back with my left hand. With my right, I reached into my holster and drew my .38.

It was a risky move, but the gangly man wasn't expecting it. If he were, he might have fired immediately at me. Now it was more complicated. The burly man grimaced and let out a painful yelp. I placed my pistol against the side of his head and fingered the trigger.

"Drop your weapon!" I ordered. "Now!"

He didn't drop his weapon. In fact, he didn't quite know what to do about this suddenly murky situation. He raised his gun in a shaky manner and pointed it at us. I moved my body behind the burly man, using him as a human shield. And I stopped pointing the gun at the side of his head. That wasn't working. The gangly man certainly wasn't thinking about dropping his pistol. If anything, he was searching to see if he could get off a clear shot at me.

"You're going to get your friend killed!" I yelled at him.

"Friend?! What friend?! I barely fucking know him!"

The gangly man was moving around, stepping gingerly to his left, trying to draw a bead on me. I positioned my body more fully behind the burly man, who kept jostling his arm, trying to break free. I jerked his arm upward again, but this time he screamed and doubled over in pain, leaving me exposed. The gangly man saw the opening, just like I saw it. He raised his gun, and I let go of my human shield. I plunged quickly to the ground. There was an orange flash and the explosive bang of a gunshot. I pulled myself quickly up on one knee. There was no time to think, only time to respond. I didn't know if I'd been hit. I extended my right arm and aimed for the middle of his body.

In my years as an officer on the LAPD, I had discharged my weapon twice. Both times I had been engaged in life-threatening encounters, and both times my response had been deadly. This was the first shooting I had been involved in as a Private Investigator, but my eye was still good. The shot hit the gangly man in the chest and he fell right over and sprawled on his back. He did not move.

Time stood still for a moment as I struggled to make

sense of what had just happened. My pulse was racing and I breathed deeply. My body gravitated back against a car. I was not paying much attention to the burly man who had stumbled a few feet and was quickly surveying the scene. He glanced at me and suddenly began to sprint away. I wheeled and aimed my gun at the fleeing man. In the background though, I was sure I saw someone walking. It distracted me, but it also provided a prescient reminder that there were bystanders nearby. I didn't know the man running away, and he certainly didn't pose a threat to me at this stage. I lowered my gun and watched him flee. The only noise I heard was the man's sneakers hitting the pavement softly. The sound grew more and more distant, until there was only an eerie silence.

*

The paramedics were the first responders, but there was no real need for them. The gangly man was dead before he'd hit the ground. I managed to leave Juan Saavedra a cryptic message on his voice mail before Building Security came over and ordered me to stay where I was. I had already holstered my .38 and didn't bother to tell them anything other than the obvious, that the dead man had indeed been shot. I spent the next few minutes leaning against the maroon van, pondering the meaning of life and waiting for the real cops to arrive.

The Santa Monica Police made it to the crime scene before the LAPD. Local law enforcement often works this way, especially when an incident happens on the border of two cities. The smaller the department, the quicker they can actually respond. Santa Monica P.D. didn't have anywhere near as much physical turf to cover. A pair of uniforms relieved me of my weapon, handcuffed my arms behind my back, and grilled me with the usual staple of questions. I told them I was a licensed Private Investigator and had a permit to carry the gun. They were duly unimpressed, so I figured I'd wait for the LAPD's Robbery-Homicide detectives to arrive before saying anything further. This wouldn't earn me any new friendships with the locals, but I had bigger priorities.

I didn't know the first pair of LAPD detectives who interviewed me; they were fairly young. They read me my Miranda rights, and I gave them my statement. For criminals wanting to avoid convictions, keeping quiet is the best protocol. Experienced felons have learned that the burden of proof is on law enforcement, and not much good can come from talking without an attorney present. Having been on both sides of the interrogation process, however, I'd learned that an innocent party can move the process along quicker by talking straight with cops. Usually, that is.

The complication I was ensnared in was as unexpected as the shooting itself. The gun being waved around by the gangly man was nowhere to be found. Maybe the burly man had grabbed it as he ran away, the events had transpired at lightning-quick speed. So at first blush, this scene had all the earmarks of a cold-blooded murder, an innocent victim gunned down by a trigger-happy former cop. Without any witnesses or evidence that the gangly man was armed, my airtight story was now sounding very squishy.

After a while, LAPD loaded me into a cruiser and we drove over to the Purdue Division. It was not the first time I had been paraded through a police station in handcuffs. It was, however, the first time I had been suspected of committing a homicide. And the facts were clear that I did kill someone today. Proving self-defense was another matter entirely. I took advantage of my one phone call, got through to Gail, and hastily explained the situation. She said she'd be on it, but certain things came first. Carla had gone home and Gail needed to find someone to look after Marcus. Getting her husband off of a murder rap would have to wait. Oddly, I understood.

"Let's go over this again," said the detective, a nicely dressed Asian man named Danny Lee. He wore a dark gray shirt and a dark blue tie. A Beretta M9 handgun was clipped to his belt.

"How many times do you need to hear my story?" I asked, knowing the answer would be as many times as he felt like. This was standard procedure. The goal was to find any inconsistency in what the suspect was saying. The more times a suspect told the story, the more opportunities would spring up for finding holes. And the better the chance for getting at the real truth.

"I just want to understand this. You got a voice mail message from a woman you'd never heard from before, calling from a blocked number, telling you to go to Laputa headquarters to meet the President of the Company."

"Not the President, he's the CEO. Apparently

President isn't the highest rank anymore in corporate America."

"Sure. But there really was no meeting, was there? It was a ruse, right?"

"Yes. Apparently someone wanted to liven up my Wednesday afternoon."

"Uh-huh. And then a man you've never seen before pulls a gun on you and orders you into his van."

"Two men. One burly, one gangly."

"Oh, right. A pair of men. So the two of them lead you to the van, but you go and beat up one of them. The big, burly one, of course. Then what happened?"

"I had him in a hammer lock and used him to shield my body in case the gangly man discharged his weapon."

"Oh. But then he *did* discharge his weapon, didn't he? Even though his friend was in the line of fire."

"Not exactly," I replied. "The gangly man said the other one wasn't really his friend."

"Of course not," the detective replied, clearly relishing the growing absurdity of my story. "Go on."

"So after the gangly man fired his weapon, I returned fire and took him down. The burly man ran off. There were passersby, so I couldn't risk discharging my weapon again."

"No, you wouldn't want to shoot an innocent person now, would you? That would be wrong."

"Uh, look, detective," I said, rubbing my face. "I understand that without his weapon, this story might appear to have a couple of pieces missing."

"A couple?!" Detective Lee exploded. "Burnside, your

story has more holes than a hunk of Swiss cheese! There are more missing pieces in your alibi than any half-witted goon could ever dream up. None of this holds water. Why don't you do yourself a favor and tell me what really happened."

"Unfortunately, I have. Honest Injun."

"Then how come we can't find the man's gun? His name, by the way, was Mike Black. Name ring a bell?"

"No. Did you run the plates on the maroon van?"

"Of course we did. And yes, he does own it. That doesn't mean he was trying to kidnap you at gunpoint."

"Why would I shoot an innocent man?" I asked.

"That's what I'd like to know," he said. "I've worked Robbery-Homicide for five years now. I've seen people get shot over a parking space. Or because someone's dog pees on their lawn. Or because they were cheering for the wrong team at a ballgame. Nothing surprises me anymore."

I kept quiet. Detective Lee was correct, there were countless inane reasons for murdering someone. But there was always an explanation, no matter how petty or stupid or pathetic that reason might be. In my case, there was only confusion, a hazy mist of what happened, and with critically important evidence missing.

A female detective walked into the interrogation room and handed Detective Lee a sheet of paper. He glanced at it and then glanced at me. The woman shot me a look that made me feel slightly lower than a cockroach, and then she exited the room.

"Well, this is interesting," Danny mused. "It says here

that Mike Black, the guy you shot, is one of your *compadres*."

"I don't have *compadres*," I said. "Not anymore."

"Sure you do. Says here Mike Black is a Private Investigator. Works out of Tarzana. "

I shrugged. "Never heard of him. But I haven't been to many club meetings."

"It also says he has a rap sheet. Man, you P.I.s are something else. To think some people actually call you detectives. You're closer to being criminals. This guy Black has been picked up for, let's see here, burglary, assault, breaking and entering, arson. At least he wasn't a former cop. I don't know how some of you clowns get licensed. Quite a brotherhood you've got there, Burnside."

"Like I said, I'm not exactly on the same side as him."

"Uh-huh. The other guy's named Chucky Flange. That name ring a bell?"

"Nope. But I'm very impressed with your ability to find this stuff out quickly."

"You think we just sit around eating doughnuts all day?" he sneered.

I looked up at the ceiling as if I were in deep thought and decided not to go forward with another smart remark. Danny Lee took a deep breath. It was a long day for him, too. He looked back down at the piece of paper and told me my attorney had arrived. A minute later, Gail Pepper entered the room and quietly sat down next to me.

"I'd like a moment alone with my client, please, Detective," she said softly.

"Sure, counselor. You working the other side of the

street these days?"

"No," she replied. "Just slumming."

Danny Lee chuckled. "Nice to see you again," he said as he walked out of the room.

"Colleague?" I asked.

"We worked a couple of cases last year."

The two of us sat there for a minute and said nothing. The silence spoke volumes. Gail was still dressed in a cream-colored business suit, a color that brought out the richness in her chestnut brown hair. But her gray eyes, the prettiest eyes I had ever gazed into, now looked sad. Sad in a way that bespoke disappointment. I might have preferred having her visibly upset. Seeing her in such a somber mood pulled at my heartstrings.

I told her what had happened. Gail listened carefully and asked a few questions. She had me state, in a very careful way, exactly what I had told the police. Finally, she started to tell me what she had learned.

"We're going to review video evidence. There are some cameras situated in the garage, although not necessarily close to where you were. I've asked one of my investigators to comb through the crime scene carefully, to see if there was any possible place the gun could be. The other person, this Chucky Flange, had a permit to carry a weapon also, so it's possible he was armed. The fact that both of them had criminal records plays in your favor, too."

"I can't believe Mike Black was a P.I."

"His license had been suspended. But yes, it is interesting how he got one in the first place."

"So what do we do now?" I asked.

"It's not what we do, it's what I do," she told me, her voice terse and withdrawn. "And how the City Attorney responds. He can't show favoritism just because I work in his office."

"I understand."

"Juan's here," she said. "I'm going to talk with him."

"Okay. Where's Marcus?"

"The neighbors are watching him. The Parkers. He'll be fine."

Gail got up and walked out of the room. The police had taken my phone and there were no windows in the office. I was left to ponder my thoughts. By my estimation, it was close to 10:00 pm. I yawned and closed my eyes. Just as I was drifting off, the door opened again, and in walked Gail, followed by Danny Lee and Juan Saavedra.

"Captain," I said, my voice a little slurred from a too-brief slumber. "It's great to see you working the night shift. I'm sure the good citizens of West Los Angeles will rest easier knowing you're on the job."

"Can you ever shut up with the wise cracks?" he snarled. "They really do get old."

"I'm not sure what else I can offer at this point."

"Look," Juan sighed, "believe it or not, I'm trying to help you here."

"Sorry. It's been a long day."

"It has. A long couple of days actually. Two homicides in two days, and you've managed to be involved in both of them. What am I supposed to think here?"

I wasn't entirely sure what I thought about all this

myself, so keeping quiet felt like a darned good idea. Juan took a seat across from me. Danny Lee stood behind him, and Gail stood next to me.

"Here's where we're at," Juan began. "Ballistics went through the garage. They didn't find Mike Black's gun. But they did find a bullet hole in a far wall, about 150 feet away. The opening was fresh, had to have been recent. They dug out a .25 slug. There was also a casing nearby."

"It looked like a cheap gun. Saturday Night Special," I commented.

"Yeah. Lucky for you. They're notorious for being inaccurate," Juan continued. "Black had a license to carry a gun, but there's no .25 registered under his name."

No wonder, I thought. I'd be embarrassed to reveal I was carrying a piece of junk like that. Although the more likely scenario was that he used a pistol that couldn't be traced. "So you can establish a gun was fired at me today."

"We can establish a gun was fired in the garage recently. Beyond that we have to use our *judgment*," he said, emphasizing the last word.

"Okay."

"And the other news I need to impart is we picked up Chucky Flange. Mike Black's partner. Yes, he was burly, wearing a black t-shirt. Just like you described."

"You were pretty quick."

"Technology," Juan said. "Couple that with stupidity and that's how we catch a lot of crooks these days. That guy Flange? What a knucklehead. After he left the garage, he tried to order a car from Uber. Only thing is, his credit card's expired. So he called five different taxi services to pick him up. I guess he figured if he called enough of them, one would show up quickly."

"Sounds like a real thinker."

"Yeah. Of course, he probably didn't figure that the cabbies cooperate with the police. Not a lot of taxi requests come out of the Laputa building, most employees drive or bike or take the bus to work. It took us like five minutes to get Flange's cell phone number and then track down his address. Lives up in Van Nuys. When we brought him in here, we did a scan on his phone. He was at Laputa this afternoon and the taxi calls were from him. Most everything you said checks out. "

"*Most* everything I said?" I asked, peering at Juan.

"Yeah, there was a slight discrepancy in your stories, though. He said that he and his colleague were unarmed and minding their own business. You made a few smart cracks and they told you to shut up. At that point, you drew your weapon and shot Mike Black on the spot. Said Black didn't have a gun. Anything you care to change in your story?"

Eight

Having been a former police officer, I have some credibility with local law enforcement. But when that's overshadowed by having been kicked off the force, the credibility starts to wane. And while neither Mike Black nor Chucky Flange were upstanding members of the community, one of them was dead and there was a gaping hole in my story. I was a person of interest because, with Mike Black's gun absent from the scene, there was no direct proof he was armed when he accosted me. Weapons used in a deadly altercation do not simply vanish into thin air. And as much as I tried to replay the scene in my mind, I kept coming back to the same stultifying conclusion. Once I shot Mike Black, the gun came out of his hand, and then it seemingly disappeared. It did not disappear, of course. The question was where did it end up. That was a question without an answer. For now, though, Captain Juan Saavedra was willing to give me the benefit of the doubt. He did advise me not to leave town.

I was released around midnight. Gail was painfully quiet on our drive home and I did not consider this a good sign. We picked up a sleeping Marcus from our neighbors and transported him to his own bed. Gail went to sleep quickly, barely saying goodnight and leaving me with the impression this day could not end soon enough. My nerves were still jangled, so I dug out a bottle of Jack Daniels and managed to throw down two fingers of

Tennessee whiskey. I finally crawled into bed but slept fitfully, dozing off for good at about 5:00 a.m., and barely hearing Gail leave for work. I woke up right before noon, just as Carla was taking Marcus to Burger King for lunch, a detail I didn't think she'd be sharing with Gail. I gave Marcus a big, long hug and told him that I loved him. He told me he wanted french fries. I declined Carla's offer to bring me back something. No part of my body was feeling in tip-top shape right now, least of all my stomach. They left, and I plopped down on the living room sofa, wanting desperately to stop thinking about last night, but knowing that wasn't about to happen.

There is something about killing another human being that changes you. I experienced this twice before. The first time came after I had been on the job with the LAPD for five years. Our unit was called to a residential location along Crenshaw in South L.A., and a man, sky high on angel dust, was swinging a knife at passersby. My partner and I both drew our weapons and repeatedly ordered him to drop the knife. But he was so drugged out, he was just in another world, one where the two uniforms in front of him might well have resembled grizzly bears. All of a sudden he made a beeline for us, knife raised and screaming incoherently, giving us no choice but to open fire.

The second incident happened about a year later. We were called to a disturbance outside a Mexican restaurant about a mile south of USC. Two men were involved in a fist fight. My partner and I broke it up, each grabbing one of the assailants. But before I could get the cuffs on him, my suspect tried to wrestle my service revolver out of its holster. In the ensuing struggle, the gun discharged and the man died immediately. He had apparently been drinking heavily that night and was obviously not in his right mind. But that didn't change the fact that by going for my gun, he took steps to put my life in jeopardy. As well as his own.

Internal Affairs investigated both episodes as was the protocol, and declared each one to be a righteous shoot. But while I.A. cleared me, my conscience did not. Even though I knew in my heart that I did the right thing, it did not spare me from the agony that comes with ending someone's life. I spent many months reliving each shooting and had to endure countless nightmares. The department assigned a psychotherapist to me each time, one of whom gave me the clinical explanation of what I was going through. Post-traumatic stress disorder. She asked if I wanted to talk about it with her, and after a too-long period of deliberation, I gave her my machismo-laced answer, which was no, not especially. These were paths I felt I needed to go down on my own. I was angry at the men who got killed, these inebriates who might have killed me if I hadn't acted quickly. Or if my weapon failed to fire properly. A life-and-death situation is just that. But I knew episodes like these didn't end when an assailant is engaged and taken down, or when the powers that be conclude their investigation. For me, that is merely one step on the trail. This was a journey that would inevitably last a while. The best thing I could do for myself was to better understand why it happened.

I drove to my office and began combing through the Internet. Mike Black had a colorful website promoting his agency, and touting his status as a "master detective." It was the type of website I had been thinking of developing, albeit mine would have more legitimate credentials. A further look into Mike Black's background revealed he was an actor by trade, although his last role listed was from six years ago. While there was no indication of his ever having been employed by any police department, he did work as a security guard for a number of private firms. His list of services included surveillance of cheating spouses, fugitive recovery and fraud investigation. It did not include kidnapping at gunpoint.

Chucky Flange did not have much of an internet presence, I only gleaned that he lived in Van Nuys and had spent at least some time in the L.A. County Jail. I was about to look up their most recent addresses when my cell phone rang. It was Gail. Her voice was muted and serious.

"Hi. Can you talk?" she asked.

"Yes. I'm at the office," I said.

"Good. I wanted to speak with you about what happened. I wasn't in a good frame of mind to do that last night."

"Me neither. Are you in a better place now?"

"Maybe a little. I apologize for doing this over the phone, but we can't discuss this in front of Marcus. This whole episode scares me. A lot. What you do and how you do it. Sweetie, it's not what I signed up for."

"You know my history. You know what I do for a living. You also know I'm exceptionally good at it."

"I do know that," she said tersely. "But there are other things you should consider. You have a son now. It's not just the two of us. I don't want Marcus growing up without a dad. Or a dad who gets involved in gunfights. Even a fistfight makes me nervous."

"I don't seek these things out," I said, and then stopped. What I told her was true in a way, but I did instigate confrontations. Sometimes I forced escalations to happen. Often it was to get people to reveal things they otherwise might not. Occasionally it was pride or stubbornness on my part. But yesterday was different.

"Is there any way you could have avoided what happened in that garage?"

I took a breath. "I honestly don't know," I said. "Once things were in motion, no. But was there a way to not let things reach that point? I have no idea. I'm not sure who was behind this. I'm not sure what their goal was, if they were trying to just scare me or if their motives were really sinister. To take me out."

"This whole case was supposed to be a simple background check."

"It was. But in the course of it, the Security Director at BMB got murdered. Was my involvement related? It's hard to see how, but I can't dismiss it. If I wasn't hired, if I didn't meet with Hector Ferris at the time I did, maybe nothing would have happened to him. But events unfolded in an odd way. At this stage, I have to assume everything was related somehow. I just don't know how."

"And you're not going to rest until you find out how," she said.

I sighed. "It's part of my makeup. Curiosity is what drives me. Why people do what they do. What they might do next. I don't like leaving stones unturned."

"Even if it puts you in harm's way."

"I try to avoid it. I'll try harder now. But this is what I do. When I was coaching football, I sometimes had sixteen hour workdays. That wasn't sustainable. I need to spend time with you and spend time with Marcus."

"I know. There are tradeoffs in a marriage. But not in a family. Marcus needs you."

"Okay," I said, not entirely sure what more I could say. "You've given me a lot to think about. But I love you and Marcus more than anything. And I want us to be okay. I'll do what I need to do."

"All right," she said and sighed. "How are you holding up with all of this?"

"It's hard. Being around death is strange. I don't know how some people do it for a living. Cops who work homicide have a type of gallows humor. It allows them to do their job without getting caught up in the horror of death. It's a coping mechanism. Basically, they use humor to help them ignore the tragedy that's staring at them."

"I think I understand. A little anyway. Let's talk more about this. Oh. One other thing. I hate to bring this up, the timing's horrible, I know. But Anna Faust set up an appointment for us with the Admissions Director at the Applewood Pre-School. There was a last-minute cancellation and she got us in for tomorrow morning. It's short notice, but people say Applewood's the best."

"Okay," I said blankly.

"You think you'll be up for doing this?" she asked.

"Yeah. I'll just let you do all the talking."

"Love you."

"Love you, too," I said and hung up. I looked down at the phone and then looked around my sparse office. I didn't have any good answers for Gail. I didn't have any good answers for myself. Mostly I had a lot of questions, ones that were still hovering, poking at me whenever my mind moved to a different subject. And as I thought about all this, I heard the doorknob turn slowly and the door began to creak. And my heart began to race like crazy, and a huge dose of adrenaline kicked in.

Scrambling haphazardly, I reached into my desk drawer. I knocked over a few things like a stapler and a paper clip dispenser and yanked out my spare .38. I pointed it at the visitor as he came into view. He was short and well-dressed and looked vaguely familiar. He put his hands up quickly when he saw I was armed.

"Whoa," he shouted. "I come in peace."

"I don't know that," I shouted, not lowering my weapon. "Tell me who you are."

"I think you know me," he said in a loud, nervous voice. "Or at least you should by now. I'm Eric Starr. You've been looking into my background."

"You're Eric Starr?" I said, dumbfounded, the gun starting to feel a little silly in my hand.

"Yes. I am. And I'll show you my I.D. if you want. But can you please put that damn thing away?"

*

The photos I had seen were admittedly a few years old. His hairline had receded a bit and a slight paunch had developed across his middle. But the intense expression was still there. Had I not been shaken by the previous day's events, I doubt I'd have provided him with such a hostile greeting.

"Sorry," I said, putting the gun back in the drawer. "Occupational hazard. I'm not used to visitors. Or surprises."

"Okay. Mind if I sit down? Promise you won't shoot me?"

"Sure, scout's honor," I said, gesturing to one of the cheap chairs facing me. "Have a seat."

Eric Starr pulled up a chair. "So. Do you mind if I ask who hired you."

"I don't mind. But I'm not going to tell you. Confidentiality and all."

"I'll pay you a million dollars," he said.

I thought about this for a moment. Eric Starr was someone who could actually afford to do that. But he was also a shrewd businessman and the information was hardly worth the price.

"You're a liar," I told him. "You wouldn't pay up."

He took this in. "That's right. I just wanted to see how you'd respond. I know BMB hired you."

"Oh, do you now?"

"Yes. I've got a few contacts here and there."

"Did you pay them a million dollars?"

He shook his head, although I doubt it was in

response to my question. "Why did you come see me yesterday? Out of the blue. Did you really think I'd fall for that line and talk to you? That someone called and said I wanted to see you?"

"Well, someone did call. And now, here you are in my office. Wanting to see *me*."

"Yes, I suppose I am."

"So what do you want?" I asked, eyeing him carefully.

"What do you think I want?" he said, using my trick of answering a question with a question. I decided to play along. It wasn't every day that a rich and famous guy stopped by my office to shoot the breeze.

"I think you want to know what I've learned," I said. "About you. About your family, your company, your dead partner. About why I shot someone to death yesterday inside your nice, clean parking garage. But mostly, I think you want to know what I'm going to do with all that information going forward."

Eric Starr processed this slowly before responding. "Yeah. That about covers it. Maybe you can tell me about what happened in the garage yesterday."

"It was all over the news. Probably on your internet site. Or don't you bother to read what's on Laputa's home page?"

"I know the public version. I'd like to know your version."

"One and the same. A couple of goons approached me. One pulled a gun and ordered me into his van. I disarmed him."

Starr frowned. "How'd you do that?"

"By shooting him in the chest. And by the way, if someone brings a .25 caliber pistol to your lost and found department, would you kindly let the police know?"

"Man, you're a real smartass," he said dryly. "All right, look. What are you going to do now?"

"Take what little I've learned, piece it together and try and make sense of it all. Or at least make things somewhat understandable."

"Do they pay you well to do this stuff?" he asked.

"How should I put this. I'm overpaid for the service I'm providing. I'm vastly underpaid for the risks I'm taking."

"I could pay you more."

"I know you could. But we've already established that you're a liar."

For the first time, Eric Starr gave what appeared to be a genuine smile. I got the feeling he wasn't used to people talking to him like this. I also got the distinct feeling that it didn't bother him. Most wealthy people I've met are impressed with themselves. Usually more than they deserve. I think back to that old line about the guy who was born on third base and thinks he hit a triple. Eric Starr may well have been born on third base. But it also struck me that he might not be thinking much about how he got there, only where he was going next.

"I have a problem," he told me.

"Don't we all."

"My problem," he continued, "is that BMB is ready to offer me the top job. But something's stopping them. I need to know if I'm in any trouble."

"What trouble could you possibly be in?" I asked.

"Nothing serious," he replied, albeit grimly.

I rolled my eyes. "Look, when a billionaire walks into my office and asks if he's in trouble, my guess is it's something serious."

"I'm not a billionaire. Not even close. And I can't talk about it."

"Because if you did, it might cost you the job with BMB. But here's a question that's been puzzling me all along. You've built something amazing in Laputa. Why give it up just to take on a corporate job where you'd be an employee, not an owner."

"A CEO of a Fortune 500 company is close to being an owner. Or maybe a king."

"Not when BMB changes CEOs every year or two," I said. "The attrition rate is staggering."

Starr shrugged. "Malcolm Taylor only lasted a year and he wound up doing all right."

"Look. Something else is going on here. If you've done your homework on me, you'll know I'm not going to let up until I find out. And if you were behind that incident in the garage yesterday, you know I don't go down easy."

He jolted upright in a hurry. "That wasn't me," he protested. "I had nothing to do with that. I'm not in the murder business."

"Tell me what happened to your partner. Jack Beale."

His eyes flashed. "That wasn't me either. I wasn't even on the boat. All I know is it was an accident."

"Convenient."

"Is that what you're thinking? That I had my partner

killed, and that I made sure I was 3,000 miles away at the time? Nothing could be further from the truth."

"I don't have anything else to go on," I shrugged.

"You need to take a good look at something," he responded.

"What's that?"

"Who stands to gain if I don't get the BMB job?"

I thought about it for a moment. A few names sprang to mind. So did the nagging suspicion that Eric Starr was suggesting a path for me to go down. He had his own agenda, and maybe something he wanted kept quiet.

"Tell me something," I said. "Are you married?"

"No. Why would I be?"

"Why not?" I responded.

"I'm having too much fun being single."

"Okay. But whenever I bring up the name Eric Starr, a lot of people make it sound like you're a womanizer. Why is that?"

"I've seen how women act when their guy's rich," he shrugged. "They spend your money and then try and mold you to their liking. If you don't give in to them, they go and make your life miserable."

"So your mantra is use them before they use you?"

"Something like that."

I looked hard at Eric and wondered what woman led him to this point. Probably his mother, this all usually starts at an early age. He had a character flaw, probably not a serious one, the question was whether the people who ran BMB would think it's serious enough to keep looking for a new CEO.

"I don't think I can help you at this stage," I said.

"Fair enough," Starr responded, and got up and walked out.

I tried to think about what I should do next, but nothing obvious crossed my mind. Sitting in my office didn't seem productive. There was one place I thought I should visit, even though I doubted my LAPD friends would approve.

It is the rare community that is named after an action hero, but Tarzana had that distinction. A suburban community located in the San Fernando Valley, it was a nice enough place to live. When Edgar Rice Burroughs chose to buy a ranch there a century ago and name it after Tarzan, it might have been a cute gesture. Why the community decided to keep the name after the author sub-divided, sold the land and departed California was not so cute. It was strange. But there were many strange things in L.A., and this would not make the top ten, or even the top hundred. And at this stage, I doubted most Angelinos even took the time to wonder about it.

Mike Black's office was located in a shabby 3-story walk-up building on Ventura Boulevard. There was a flower shop on the ground floor, adjacent to a liquor store. The directory next to the stairwell listed a real estate agency, a funeral parlor, an adult film production company called Woo Woo Productions, and a detective agency called Black Investigations.

There was no yellow police tape across the door, so LAPD had not bothered to send anyone here yet. If they planned to at all. Approaching the office door, I slipped on a pair of latex gloves. I tried the doorknob, and, not surprisingly, it was locked. What was surprising though, was the absence of any frame or shield. There was nothing inhibiting me from simply sliding a credit card into the latch, lifting the door slightly and jimmying it open. It was Burglary 101 and the entire process took less than three seconds and made virtually no noise. If anyone else was in the building they hadn't heard. Even if they had, my guess was they wouldn't have cared.

Mike Black's office had a reception area with an empty desk. The office door was open and I walked through. His desk had a few papers on it and a docking station for his laptop, which was missing. Next to the desk was a gray file cabinet with four drawers. It was locked, but the key was lying in the top desk drawer. Security was obviously not a priority for Mr. Black.

I went through the entire file cabinet and couldn't help but notice folders labeled with the names of various large companies, as well as a few with some famous celebrities. I finally found what I was after in the bottom drawer. A manila folder with the name BMB on the tab. The folder showed signs of wear, but when I pulled it out, the folder contained nothing. No invoices, no photos, no notes. It was wrinkled and had been handled sufficiently enough to indicate that at one point it must have been very full. Apparently, someone had gotten here before me.

Nine

None of Mike Black's neighbors in the building had witnessed anyone coming in or out of his office today. Or yesterday. The owner of Woo Woo Productions casually mentioned Black had been cast in one of their films last year, but they hadn't been impressed with his acting ability. I wasn't sure how much talent a porn actor needed beyond the obvious physical attributes, but apparently Mike Black did not get any callbacks for future roles. The clerk at the liquor store confirmed Black as a regular, but aside from learning his preference for mixing cheap vodka with Red Bull, I had few clues to help in my fledgling investigation.

I pondered my next stop, deciding to call ahead and see if it was worth what would be an hour-plus drive. When I phoned Benjamin Starr's home, the person answering was clearly not Benjamin Starr. A few questions revealed the elder Starr was in New York on business, and that his wife had tagged along to visit the swank shops along Fifth Avenue. That was just what I wanted to hear. What I did not want to hear, though, was my phone buzzing immediately after I hung up. I had just merged onto the welcomed path of clear traffic on the 101 freeway. I glanced down at a brief text. Nick Roche wanted to see me.

The executive tower loomed over the BMB lot. It was a blue and gray glass building, with enough angles jutting out to make it look artistic. The interior lobby featured a huge atrium with a glass ceiling wide enough to allow a vast amount of light to pour in. So much so, that the effect was not unlike a greenhouse, a little warm and more than a little dank. It was the type of lobby most likely designed by a smarmy architect who would never have to sit in it. Large wall vents blew cold air down mercifully, but it was still uncomfortable.

After a twenty minute wait, Nick Roche's young assistant arrived, and led me up to the top floor and into his office. Roche was on the phone, feet up on the window sill, gazing aimlessly across the western horizon. It had been a few days since our weekend rainstorm, and layers of smog had started to form again. You could still make out the Pacific, a bit fuzzy in the distant sky, but it made for a very different view than the one just a few days ago. But to me, everything felt different from a few days ago. Roche motioned for me to sit and quickly finished his call.

"Burnside, thanks for coming."

"Sure," I said.

"I'd like a progress report," he declared, and his mouth grew stern. "And an explanation for how a simple background check could lead to two people getting killed."

"Good question. I'm glad I wasn't one of them. And thank you for your concern about my welfare."

"Oh. Yes. Sorry about that," he muttered, his executive posture moving down a notch.

"To be perfectly honest, I've been wondering how a background check could morph into this, too. So have the police. I'm sure they paid you a visit."

"They did. You know, you shouldn't have given them my name."

I peered at Roche. "The police wanted to know who at BMB hired me," I said, my voice rising. "There are some things I don't keep from the authorities. But I'm also surprised you aren't expressing concern about your Security Director getting run down like a dog in front of his own house."

"Look. I know this has been a rough time for you, but I don't like your tone," Roche said, the indignation growing in his voice. "You make it sound like I had something to do with all this."

"Did you?"

"Of course not. Don't be ridiculous."

"Well, tell me something." I asked. "What do you think Patty Muckenthaler's role could have been here?"

"Patty? Who knows. Why are you even asking about Patty?" he said as he reached inside his desk for a pack of cigarettes. He flipped one out, lit it and looked at me. "Yes, I'm aware smoking's against the rules. Some habits are hard to break."

"I know. It's easier to break rules. The other day, Patty was meeting with Hector when you introduced us. Hector made a vague insinuation that she was involved in a sexual harassment issue. But that Patty wasn't the one being harassed. A little strange, don't you think?"

Roche took a long drag on his cigarette and pondered this. The other day he looked rather cerebral as he took a long pull and then slowly exhaled a steady stream of smoke. Now it just seemed like an act.

"Maybe," he sighed. "But this is a hard conversation to have, all things considered. And I'd like you to respect the confidentiality here. It's a very sensitive subject."

"Go on," I said.

"It has to do with Kitty Strong. She works for Patty in Production."

I took this in. "Does this person know her husband weighs 260 pounds and has a problem controlling his temper?"

"I don't know," Roche said wearily. "And in this business, some people don't care. But I have a personal interest in this issue. As you know, Kitty's my sister-in-law. My wife's sister."

"Has the offending party been notified?" I pressed.

"It's a little complicated."

"How so?"

"We have doubts that harassment was going on. At least not in the typical sense."

I shook my head. Things weren't making sense. But precious little about this case was making sense. "I don't get it."

"There's something called third-person sexual harassment. Let's say I'm in the lobby and I put my arms around a woman, and embrace her for longer than might be appropriate. And instead of getting upset, the woman tells me that it feels good. You'd think there's no sexual harassment going on, right? No one's being violated. But what if another employee were nearby and witnessed this. If they felt offended, they could claim third-person sexual harassment. That person would be the victim."

"All right," I said, nodding. "Sounds like Kitty was receptive to someone's advances."

"You don't say," he remarked, blowing some smoke up at the ceiling.

"Who else was involved?"

"It doesn't matter. The incident happened a while ago, but the third person is still filing a grievance. And these things can turn into lawsuits, and then everyone in town starts talking about it. Jay's a public figure, I know this would be devastating to him. And our image would take a hit. There aren't many winners here."

"So you're trying to keep a lid on things."

"Best I can. And with Hector getting killed, it just adds to the mess."

"That's what's so puzzling," I said. "Why would someone want Hector out of the way?"

"One of the detectives that spoke to me thought it could have been another cop. I guess Hector didn't win any popularity contests at the LAPD."

"No he didn't," I said. "And I've also been wondering if it could have been another cop. But things just don't point in that direction."

"Uh-huh," Roche said and took another puff. "You know, I need to ask you about something else. The Eric Starr investigation."

"Ah. The thing I was actually hired for."

"Yes. Where are you on that?"

"Haven't gotten very far."

"Are you kidding me?" he said disgustedly.

"Well, after a couple of thugs tried to kidnap me in the

Laputa parking garage yesterday, I managed to shoot one of them. I assume that counts as working on your assignment. I've also been spending a lot of time with the police the past few days. So I'm not exactly going over to Venice Beach and playing volleyball."

"Yes, yes, I know," he said, waving a hand apologetically.

"I did find out a few things, though. Starr was arrested for assault a couple of years ago. Victim was the wife of his business partner. Charges later dropped. You know about the partner disappearing from his yacht, right?"

"Yes, the drowning. But I was unaware of the assault charge against Eric."

"And apparently Starr filed a restraining order against the woman."

"Interesting. It appears like you've been working on this case, after all."

"I was actually on my way down to Irvine when you called," I said, ignoring the crack. "I'm planning to interview his brother. I understand Eric hired him into Laputa a few years ago and then terminated him."

"Fired his own brother?" Roche said, eyebrows raised.

"Apparently so. Although I don't imagine that would disqualify him from being hired here."

No," Roche said, stabbing his cigarette out in an ashtray. "I suppose it wouldn't. Not at all."

*

The freeway traffic was still light on the way down to

Irvine. I reached the Starr residence and parked a block away, ever mindful I had an arrest warrant still outstanding. The late afternoon sunlight was becoming diffuse, a dark, distant cloud cover was forming, but the temperature was still a pleasant 72 degrees. Lanny Starr obviously thought it was warm enough. When he answered the door, he was dressed in shorts and flip flops.

"Yeah?" he said intelligently.

I flashed my fake P.I. badge, which was nothing more than a shiny gold shield that said I was a Los Angeles Private Investigator, with the number 4040 engraved in blue. I chose the number 40 because it was my jersey number when I played for USC. The badge really did look a bit like a gold shield that an actual LAPD detective might possess, and it was handy enough to fool most people. Especially when I flashed it quickly. If the person asked to see it again, I would hand over my real P.I. license, but that didn't happen often. The person needed to be sharp enough to question my credentials.

"Are you Lanny Starr?" I asked, pretty sure I had the answer.

"Uh-huh," Lanny responded, blinking a few times. He looked like he was about 25, not much taller than his brother, but with a more sizable gut.

"Listen," I said, putting the shield away quickly, "I'm an investigator and I'm looking into some criminal activity up in West L.A. It involves your brother Eric. It's serious. We need to talk."

"Whaaa... ?" he said, struggling to make sense of this. His eyes had a reddish tinge, and he looked mildly stoned.

That might or might not be beneficial to me; it depended on how much and how long he had been smoking.

"May I come in?" I asked. "It won't take long."

"Uh, I don't know... "

"Listen," I said with a degree of urgency. "You're not in any trouble. And I don't care what you've been doing today. I just need to ask you a few questions. Won't take long."

He processed this for a few seconds and finally let me enter. The foyer opened up to a spacious great room, with a spiral staircase off to the right. To the left was a den, where Lanny lead me. The faint smell of marijuana smoke lingered in the air. I noticed a blue plastic bong sitting on the carpeted floor, placed to the side of the couch. He sat down on the couch. I sat in an easy chair next to him. A 60-inch TV was mounted across the room and a single video game controller sat on a marble-and-glass coffee table.

"So, uh, what's this about my brother?" Lanny asked.

"Yes," I said, wondering if his being partially stoned would loosen his tongue or make him paranoid. "You worked for Eric at Laputa for a while. Can you tell me about it?"

"Uh, well, yeah. I worked there for a year. Now I don't."

"Right," I said. "And then you were let go. What happened?"

Lanny hesitated for a moment. "Why are you asking me this?"

"It's important," I said brusquely, hoping my

professional demeanor would be all the detail I'd need to share for the time being. Sometimes when you speak in a grave tone and maintain the utmost seriousness, a callow witness will take on a similar disposition. "It really is. Critically important, in fact."

"Oh, okay," he said, although I wasn't quite sure whether he believed me. Or even understood. But no matter. His acquiescence was what I needed. "Well, it kind of pissed me off. Yeah, I wasn't doing a lot of work, but no one else there was. It was kind of a party atmosphere. I guess I didn't always make it into the office. Even still, when your brother's running the company, you figure you'd get treated differently. My brother has his own set of rules."

"Totally understand," I said sympathetically, although I wondered if firing an employee like this wasn't the worst move an executive could make, brother or not.

"And there was a lot of stuff going on with his partner's crazy-ass wife."

"Oh?" I said, rolling this around in my mind for a moment. "Jack Beale, the guy who drowned. What happened there?"

Lanny shrugged. "No one knows for sure. One moment he was sitting with his wife, Darcy, on the bow of the yacht. Glanced back a little later and he wasn't. Simple as that."

"You were on the boat that day?"

"Uh-huh."

"You think there was any foul play?"

"Huh?"

"Do you think someone pushed him in?" I asked, reminding myself that patience was supposedly a virtue.

"Aw man, you're making me feel bad," Lanny said.

"Sorry," I said as sincerely as I could muster. "But as I said, this is important."

He shook his head. I half expected to hear something rattle. "I really don't know," he replied, sounding a little more coherent. "The waves were choppy that day, the boat was moving around a lot. I could see him falling in. But push him over the edge? Be a dumb thing to do. I first thought maybe his wife could have maybe done it, but no. Nothing in it for her. Darcy wound up getting cut out, not even getting Jack's shares. Eric ran the company from then on, but Laputa was never the same. No one would have pushed Jack in. Unless they wanted the company to fail. And everyone on the boat that day worked for Laputa. Or I guess maybe their spouse did. Wouldn't have made sense."

"No, it wouldn't have."

"Funny thing, though."

"What's that?" I asked.

"Nearly everyone who was on the boat that day was gone from the company within a few months. Including me. Weird, you know?"

"Very weird," I repeated, a little surprised that he was being as forthcoming as he was. I didn't want to say anything that might make him stop sharing. "But you said something interesting a minute ago. That people don't do a lot of work at Laputa. What's that about?"

"Yeah, it was crazy. People would screw around all

day. It was just one big party. I mean, some people worked, but there were a lot of people that just took up space. Surfed the Internet, posted on Facebook, were on the phone a lot. It's an open office, everyone's in cubicles, so there's no privacy. Everyone sees everything, but no one really cared."

"Not even Eric?"

"Especially not Eric. He was always hitting on women in the office, flying around the country, getting his name in the paper. When Jack was there, Jack ran the show. Eric would come up with wild ideas, like turning Laputa into a TV channel, an online shopping site, a dating service. But Jack was the one who made all these things work. Or he told Eric they couldn't do it. With Jack gone, there was no one to stand up to Eric. No one there who could say no. And no one to run the office."

"What happened with his wife, Darcy? You said she got cut out."

"Oh yeah," Lanny smiled. "She was really ticked she got nothing. Or I guess she'll have to wait a few years for it. And she hated Eric. They didn't respect each other. It got nasty. One day she even took a swing at him."

"I thought Eric was the one who got charged with assault."

"Yeah. Not surprising the police thought Eric would be the instigator. They dropped the charges when they looked at her hand and saw the knuckles were scraped, plus he had a cut over his eye."

"Why do you think she took a swing at him?"

"Like I said, Darcy was ticked. She thought when Jack

died, she'd get his piece of the company. But I guess you can't rule someone dead without a body. Also, Eric and Jack had a written agreement that if one wasn't around, whatever, the other partner would take over control of Laputa. Darcy has some money, sure. But Eric got the company. Funny thing, huh?"

"How's that?" I asked.

"Eric got what he wanted. Control. And then the company started going into the ground."

I didn't understand this. "I thought Laputa was doing well."

"Everyone thinks so. But it's not. And that's why he wants to go to BMB."

"You know about that."

"Sure," Lanny said. "My dad told me. Eric doesn't want to be around when the bottom falls out. Laputa is rotting from the inside."

"Why isn't he trying to stop it then?" I asked.

"What makes you think he isn't the one ripping it apart? It doesn't take much, you know. An accountant with a spreadsheet can steal more than a hundred men with guns."

"I think I've heard that line before. Or something like it," I frowned.

Lanny shrugged. "I think it's from an old video game I used to play."

"Okay. And you think Laputa's going down the tubes. And that's the reason Eric's looking to bail?"

"That's part of it. But I'm not sure how well you know Eric. He's really competitive. If he's being considered for something big, he'll do whatever it takes to get it. It's all about the game, and the rules are always changing. For Eric, the only thing worse than not getting what he wants, is seeing someone else get it."

Ten

The sun was starting to set as I drove away from Irvine. I left Lanny Starr to go back to indulging in whatever mind-numbing activity he was engaged in before I arrived. I hadn't eaten much today, and maybe the lingering smell of weed was having an effect on me, but strong hunger pangs began to set in. I stopped at a gas station and bought a Milky Way bar, the first bite of which made me practically swoon, and I quickly rated it as among the best tasting treats I had had in quite a while. That would at least temporarily quell the hunger and get me home in one piece, although the thickening rush-hour traffic made the drive interminably long.

By the time I arrived back at our house, Gail had started making dinner. Marcus celebrated my arrival with a booming, "Daddy's home!" which filled my soul with joy. I lifted him up over my head, gave him a sky hug and suggested we go investigate what Mom was making for dinner.

Gail, with her long brown hair tied back into a ponytail, was hunched over a counter, chopping some vegetables. In a large pan sat a sizzling puddle of olive oil and a clump of minced garlic, with a steaming pot of penne pasta nearby. With Marcus in my right arm, I put my left around Gail's waist and hugged her gently. She stopped, leaned back and let me kiss her. Not wanting to miss out on the action, Marcus wrapped his arms around both of us.

"Family hug," I said.

"It feels good," she responded, and she smiled for what seemed like the first time in two days.

We ate dinner, and afterwards I played catch with Marcus in the living room, using an extra-soft pink rubber ball. After a few minutes, Chewy got wind of what we were doing and bounded over. We quickly made her monkey in the middle. It took half a dozen throws before Marcus dropped one, giving Chewy the opportunity to grab the ball in her mouth and dart out of the living room. Marcus immediately began to chase her with me in tow, making sure he went for the ball and not the dog's tail. It mattered not. Chewy had changed the rules of the game and would not let anyone catch her. My phone rang, and after looking down to see who it was, I motioned for Gail to take over as referee. I sensed the LAPD would want my full attention.

"Yes?" I began.

"Burnside."

"That's me."

"It's De Santos. Listen. I have some good news."

"That's always better than the alternative, Roberto."

"Uh-huh. Hey, I wanted to give you a follow-up on Chucky Flange. He finally dropped his story that you pulled a gun on him and Black for no reason."

"Good. You beat the confession out of him?"

"That's a little too old-school for us. We got some video footage in the garage. It's grainy and from a distance, but it clearly shows you were the one with your hands raised, and Black pointing a gun at you. I swear, it looked like some kind of a gangster scene from an old movie."

"And to think Danny Lee doubted I was telling the truth."

"Yeah. Something else came out of that video. After you fired at Mike Black, he fell backwards and the gun flew out of his hand. Went right into a pickup truck next to him. We couldn't get a read on the plate, but I sent someone over to the Laputa garage today and they looked in all the pickup beds. Sure enough, it was in one of them, a .25 ACP. Owner of the truck works for Laputa, he didn't even realize it was in there."

"So you got a match with the bullet you found in the wall?"

"Yup. We gave both to Forensics and they confirmed it. Had Mike Black's prints all over them. Everything was just like you said. We have to review all this with the City Attorney, but it looks like you're off the hook."

"Good. Anything you learn about Flange?"

"He kept denying he was a party to this. Said he met Mike Black a month ago at the gym. Black hired him a couple of times. Mostly to accompany him when he needed to serve papers or just show some muscle. But he said this was the first time he was involved in anything criminal. Swears he wouldn't have done it if he had known."

"He have much of rap sheet?"

"Nothing to speak of. Got picked up for a DUI, couple of bar fights. Just a local meathead."

"I don't suppose he said who contacted Mike Black

and gave the order to grab me."

"Nope. His story is that Black called him and said he needed some help right away. Black picked him up and the two drove down to Laputa together. It checks out. But we don't have much to hold him on. The City Attorney said there just wasn't enough to implicate him in a kidnapping case. I suppose we could charge him with lying to the police, but the jails around here are already too full. I'm sure we could charge a lot of people with that."

"Sure," I said, not wanting to press the issue.

"So we're going to let Flange walk. This case is wrapped up as far as we're concerned."

I thanked Roberto and hung up. The LAPD was considering this a closed case. But for me it was far from closed. Someone wanted to send me a message. Maybe a stern warning. Or maybe they really wanted to murder me. Mike Black was gone, but the person giving the order was still out there. They knew me, they knew I was investigating Eric Starr and they sent me to Laputa to get kidnapped and possibly killed. And I didn't have any idea who they were. Or whether they would strike again.

*

I slept fitfully again that night, waking up a number of times, drenched in sweat. It was not because of any nightmares, but when I woke up at 2:30 a.m. I was wide awake all of a sudden. I went into the den and read a little, and then watched the highlights of Day 1 of the NCAA basketball tournament on ESPN. UC-Irvine's first-round matchup was unfortunately against top-seeded Duke, and the Anteaters were clobbered 88-49. I tuned in to part of an old movie before my body signaled it was willing to rest for a while. I snoozed until 6:30 a.m. when some tiny strands of sunlight began sneaking in through the bedroom window. I thought absently about who I needed to talk with today, when I suddenly remembered the preschool appointment Gail had mentioned. She had said Anna Faust would be there to provide the introduction to the Admissions Director. She had also asked me to try and stay very positive about all of this.

"They're really interviewing us, sweetie," Gail had said. "Anna told me we should hang on every word they say like it's the gospel. And don't give them a reason to think we're anything but completely supportive of their program. That's how people get accepted."

"All right," I gulped, hoping I would have the temerity to say as little as possible. There was much about this process that I was finding distasteful.

The Applewood Preschool was ironically located down the street from my old apartment building in Santa Monica. It was a small, colorful structure with a large play area; the sounds of happy children shrieking had become a staple of the neighborhood. But I recalled the most notable thing about Applewood occurred around 3:00 p.m. every day, when a long line of Mercedes, Range Rovers, and other luxury vehicles, some driven by celebrities, lined the alley to pick up their kids.

"I am so glad you could be here on such short notice,"

Anna exclaimed as she led us into the Admissions Director's office. "Rachel, this is the wonderful couple I was telling you about. I'd like you to meet Mr. and Mrs. Burnside. This is Rachel McAfee."

Anna excused herself and said she'd speak with us afterward. A smiling college-aged assistant named Bethany led Marcus by the hand to take him on what she described as a "play date" with some wonderful children. We all smiled and sat down. Rachel McAfee was in her fifties, attractive, and wore dark slacks, an expensive pink polo shirt and a stone-washed denim jacket. She had the relaxed look of someone who was accustomed to being showered with attention.

"I must admit," she began. "You're very lucky. We don't typically have openings for our middle-aged preschoolers."

"Middle-aged?" I asked.

"Yes, well, Marcus will be middle-aged next semester. It's a three-year program, and you're applying for year two. We normally begin the application process right after Labor Day, and within a week we've reached our limit. So you see, having an opening in March is highly unusual."

Gail jumped in and lit up her million-dollar smile. "We're very grateful you're considering us. Steve Reinhardt and his wife say the most wonderful things about your program."

"Yes, I see you work for the City Attorney. Their youngest is graduating in June. He's been accepted at Carlton Elementary for kindergarten. I'm sure you know that's a feeder school to Harvard-Westlake. We take pride in our students ending up at the top prep schools on the west coast."

I listened absently as Gail turned on the charm offensive and Rachel responded positively. My role was going to have to be the strong, silent type, especially since my main questions were wrapped around what all of this would cost. As a well-paid football coach, the price of things had become secondary to pleasing my family. As a struggling private investigator, who just commissioned his first paying gig in two months, the cost of things had begun to rise in importance.

"So is Marcus reading yet?" Rachel asked.

"He's started to," Gail said proudly, and I looked to see if her fingers were crossed. "In fact, he's reading in English and Spanish."

"Well, that's very good," she responded. "You know, some of our children are reading in Mandarin now."

I considered this, realizing the only Spanish I could read was from what little I remembered from high school, and the only Chinese I knew was from the menu at Hunan Taste. I picked up a brochure from the table next to me and began to skim through it. The cost of tuition was $2,500 a month, which was higher than our mortgage. On one page it listed all the parents who had donated to Applewood's charity foundation, and how much they had given. Some of the donations were well over $10,000. I tightened my grip on the brochure. I was entering a world totally foreign to me, one where I sensed that owning a summer home and jetting overseas for a long weekend was more common than not.

"Interesting," Gail said and looked at me, her eyes narrowing as if to tell me to start paying attention and engaging. "We'll need to explore that."

"Absolutely," I managed, wondering just what I was agreeing to. "It's a wonderful idea."

"So tell me," Rachel asked. "How would you describe Marcus?"

At that point, I returned to my role of being quiet and letting my beautiful, articulate wife take over. She spoke expansively about the advanced social skills Marcus possessed, his ease with other kids and his love of performing. He was into oil painting and taking piano lessons. I listened with interest, wondering just how much I had missed during the past three years as an overly-involved football coach. I knew Gail didn't lie, but I also knew she had a lawyer's knack for stretching the truth until it could become distended beyond recognition.

We answered a few more questions and Rachel McAfee appeared quite satisfied. At that point, Bethany returned with Marcus, and Rachel asked him how he liked the school.

"It was okay," he said with a shrug. "Do I have to build pots?"

Rachel smiled. "I'm sure you'll love our pottery-making class. We're the only preschool in the area that has one."

Gail said that sounded so wonderful, and I had to repress the urge to suggest she herself might be the one more interested in attending Applewood. In fairness, I wasn't sure if she was simply extending flattery.

We finished the interview and were told that all we needed to do now was fill out the application and they would make a decision in a few weeks. There were other candidates, but Rachel McAfee thought we would be an exceptionally good fit, and mentioned Gail's boss's name again. We left the preschool and saw Anna Faust sitting in her Mercedes, chatting with someone on her cell phone.

Gail and I had driven separately, so we agreed to talk more about this in the evening and she took Marcus home. I waited for Anna to finish her conversation and then motioned to her that we needed to speak. I knew Gail wouldn't be pleased with what I was about to ask, but some things were more important to me than getting our son admitted into an elite preschool. And a certain proletariat part of me had a curious desire to blow the whole application process to smithereens.

"So how did it go?" she asked.

"Fine, it's a nice school."

"Well, I just got off the phone with Rachel and she's duly impressed with you. I think you're in."

"Great, great," I said, trying to figure out a way to steer the conversation elsewhere. "Listen, Anna. I need to ask you something. Unrelated to schools. It's about Laputa. It's a little difficult, but I need your help."

"Oh?"

"You mentioned you worked in HR there. Human resources. I'm doing on an investigation regarding Laputa. It's in conjunction with a law enforcement issue."

"I'm not sure how much help I can provide," she said warily.

"Let me ask you something. How much interaction did you have with Eric Starr?"

"Not much. He wasn't usually around."

"And his brother, Lanny?"

"Thankfully, no. He wasn't much use to anyone."

"And Jack Beale?"

"Say, just what is this all about?"

"A client of mine, a Fortune 500 company, is doing a background check on Eric. They're considering him for a very high level job, running a large organization," I said, eyeing her. "Does that surprise you?"

"No, not in the slightest. I'm surprised he hasn't tried to get out of Laputa before this."

"Why's that?" I blinked.

"The company is living off of their reputation. Running on fumes, actually. It's only a matter of time before it falls apart. Eric's a prime reason."

"Didn't he start the company?"

"He started it, but Jack Beale's the one who built it. He was the brains, Eric was the mouth. Oh, look, I suppose there's a gift in being able to promote and market a company, and Eric had that talent. But all of his grand ideas were made operational by Jack."

"So you might say when Jack fell into the water, the company went with it."

"You certainly might," she said.

"What else can you tell me about Eric. Or Laputa?"

"Honestly, I can't share much more. I've been gone for a while, I left the company shortly after that incident with Jack happened. I was laid off."

"Sorry to hear that," I said.

"And the terms of my agreement prevent me from discussing certain things."

"Oh?"

Anna shrugged. "Let's just say the severance package was very nice."

Eleven

I sat in my Pathfinder and rolled Anna's comments around in my mind. She wasn't forthcoming with anything further regarding the boating accident, and no amount of prodding was going to dislodge anything more today. In fact, she told me she had probably said too much as it was.

I opened up my iPad and turned my attention to Eric, and in particular, his equity position in Laputa. It took some digging, but I found a few websites that reported when executives were selling shares of company stock. This disclosure was required by law, but it often got pushed off of the front pages by more lurid news. One Wall Street analyst noted Eric had dumped a sizable number of shares, but also divulged that he was also about to buy an estate in Napa Valley. I guess Eric didn't have a spare $85 million lying around.

I drove a few blocks away from the Applewood Preschool. The neighborhood north of Montana Avenue was an exclusive one. Wide, spacious streets were lined with beautiful homes, fronted by well-tended lawns. Healthy-looking joggers trotted along the sidewalk next to well-dressed people walking well-coiffed dogs on retractable leashes. But in the years I lived near here, I had been inside just one of these stellar homes, and that was only because of my friendship with Crystal Fairborn. I had no regrets about buying a small house and moving to Mar Vista, but I still looked ever-so-fondly, and occasionally wistfully, back on my life in Santa Monica.

Darcy Beale lived in a Craftsman home that was probably constructed a century ago, but it had since been tastefully, and expensively, updated. There were seven steps leading up to the front door, and the house was framed by a wraparound veranda. The exterior featured an intricate collection of small teakwood slats forming a patchwork design. A series of low-pitched gabled roofs topped both the first and second stories. It was the type of home you might see pictures of in an issue of *Architectural Digest*.

I rang the bell, and a woman in her early 30s answered it. She was tall, blonde and athletic. Wearing a white cotton top and black spandex, she looked like she was about to go work out. Or maybe she had just returned.

"Yes?" she asked, leaning forward inquisitively.

"Darcy Beale?" I asked, flashing my fake gold shield. "May I have a word with you?"

She blinked a few times. "What is this about?"

"Strictly routine," I said in my most officious voice. "It concerns Eric Starr."

The name got her attention and her eyes darkened. But she apparently had a sufficient amount of curiosity, enough to invite me inside.

"Nice place," I said as I walked into the stunning living room. Polished oak floors, high beamed ceilings and a limestone-rimmed fireplace would grab any visitor's attention. Wide bay windows allowed a flood of light inside. I decided this was the type of house I would buy if I ever won the lottery.

"Please have a seat," she said coolly. "What's your name?"

"Burnside," I responded, moving onto a couch facing the fireplace. "Sorry. I guess I was distracted by your home."

"It is lovely, isn't it?" she said unsmiling, as she sat in a chair next to me. "But what is this about Eric?"

"I'm doing an investigation. I have a client who's interested in hiring him to head up a large company. They want to learn more about him before they offer him the job."

"Really?" she said. "Who?"

"I'm not at liberty to say yet. But I can probably tell you at some point. What do you think? Eric being a CEO of a Fortune 500 company?" I asked, figuring an open ended question might elicit some venom. Which might lead to some hidden details. But none were forthcoming. Darcy Beale looked across the room. She was either deep in thought or trying to figure out how best to phrase something.

"I think it sounds like a great move," she finally said. "Eric is eminently qualified."

Now it was my turn to stop and think. This wasn't quite the answer I was expecting. "I'm a little surprised by that," I admitted.

"You needn't be," she said. "Eric and my husband took Laputa and nurtured it into something. Something big. It's not surprising Eric would want to move on. This is what people like Eric do. They need new challenges. I think it's healthy."

Maybe it was. But it felt odd coming from Darcy. And it did not feel genuine. Having served with the LAPD for 13 years, I had developed a strong inkling for when people weren't telling me the truth. It was something of an innate job requirement, the type of sixth sense that can sometimes save a cop's life.

"How involved were you with Laputa?" I asked.

"Behind the scenes, mostly. Helping Jack with advice. His success was my success."

"I'm sorry about what happened to him," I said. I would have liked to have probed her on what indeed happened that day on the yacht, but I doubted it would bear any fruit. And I already had doubts about Darcy Beale's honesty.

"Of course," she said, looking down. "I miss him greatly. He was a saint."

I nodded, albeit warily. When a loved one passes, it's true that the hard times are often forgotten and the fond memories are the ones that linger. "Can you tell me a little about Jack and Eric's relationship?"

"It was great," she said, looking up at me. "They were perfectly suited to be partners. Eric was the front man, he marketed the company, Jack ran the day-to-day. It was a marriage made in startup heaven. As I'm sure you know, the company did incredibly well."

"How about your own relationship with Eric?"

With that, she stopped being so effusive and retreated back into thinking mode. I waited. Finally she started to speak again. "It was all right as long as Jack was there as a buffer. With Jack gone, Eric and I ... had disagreements.

Apparently the two of them had a secret arrangement where one would get control of the company if the other wasn't there. I had no idea they agreed to that."

"Jack never told you about that detail."

"No," she said tersely. "He didn't. Never said a word."

"Do you think it was a legitimate agreement?"

Darcy Beale's mouth grew tight. "I don't know."

"And you confronted Eric."

She peered at me. "How do you know this?"

"It's on the police blotter. Matter of public record that he hit you. Did he?"

"Of course he hit me. Didn't you read the report?"

"Did you hit him first?" I asked.

Her mouth opened in surprise for a brief moment and then she began to sneer. "Of course not. That's outrageous. That's incomprehensible. Why ... why are you asking me this?"

"Eric filed a restraining order against you. Things don't usually work that way, especially if he were the one who hit you."

"No, I suppose they don't. Eric ... we argued. I felt I should have a role at Laputa. Even just to secure Jack's legacy. But he wouldn't hear of it. Eric ordered me out of his office."

"After he hit you?"

"Yes ... I mean, no. I'm getting confused. He grabbed me and I hit him back."

"Hit him back?"

"Oh," she said wearily. "I don't know what good it will do to rehash all this. What's done is done."

"All right," I said. "But one other thing. Were you aware of a woman named Wanda who worked at Laputa?"

Darcy stiffened. "I was. That tart tried to ruin my marriage. When I got wind of it, she was gone."

"You had her fired?"

"No," she smiled cleverly. "I don't do those sorts of things. I heard she had overstayed her visa, so I reported her to the INS. She was deported back to wherever the hell she came from. Good riddance."

"What about Eric's relationships with women at Laputa?"

Darcy shrugged. "He screwed anything he could get his hands on. For him, Laputa was a candy store where he had a free account to snap up whatever he wanted."

"Anyone in particular?"

She shrugged. "No. He wasn't particular."

I rose, thinking I had mined about all I could here, including Darcy's anger. I stood there for a moment, marveling at just how beautiful the house was.

"You really do have a nice home. But I want to ask you one more thing."

"What now?" she asked, some exasperation forming in her voice.

"If Eric leaves, who would run the company?"

Darcy shrugged. "Eric still has a controlling interest. He gets to decide that. Unless he sells his equity position. His stock."

"Then what happens?"

"Then," she said, her eyes shining, "things become interesting."

*

I thanked Darcy for her time, even though she probably generated as many questions for me as she did answers. I thought about what to do next, and the only thing that sprung to mind was getting a caffeine jolt. I arrived back at my office, armed with a *venti* cup of Starbucks Italian roast. It was dark and bold, and while it wasn't quite up to the level of French roast, it packed a nice caffeine wallop. For today, that's what mattered most.

As I pulled into the garage beneath my office building, I noticed someone familiar, a young man about to climb into a nicely appointed car parked in one of the visitor's spaces. Adam Gee didn't notice me, so I tapped the horn. He looked up from the black BMW 740 and stopped.

"You just in the neighborhood?" I asked.

"Oh, Mr. Burnside. I was hoping to see you. I dropped a package off. It has the contract, as well as something else Mr. Taylor wanted you to look at."

"Thanks," I said, giving his car the once over. "You drive in style."

He looked almost apologetic. "At times. I own a 15 year-old Ford Explorer. This is my boss's car. One of the perks of the job. I get to take it out once in a while. But it comes at a price."

"What's that?"

"I usually have to chauffer him around."

"There are worse things than driving an expensive BMW."

He smiled in agreement and waved.

A parcel was indeed waiting for me. The logo for Celestial Productions was in the upper left-hand corner, and it had a Century City address. I slit it open and pulled out a couple of documents, one being a contract calling for me to be paid $10,000 for technical assistance and consulting. The other was a script for a movie called *Day Watch*. Oddly, there was no writer listed. I opened the script and turned to the last page to see how long it was. It turned out to be a healthy 119 pages, which, even to my amateur's knowledge, translated to a two-hour movie. I also noted the final scene had a guy named D.J. pointing his .44 pistol at an Officer Krumm and saying the words, "Goodbye, you punk," right before he pulled the trigger and splattered the policeman's brains along the outfield wall of Dodger Stadium. I tossed the script, along with the contract, into the trash.

I sipped on the coffee and thought about my next visit. It had only been a couple of days since the tragedy, but I needed to speak with Hector Ferris's widow. This was a delicate situation. She might be very willing to talk, or she might be extremely offended, and I had no way of knowing. Nick Roche told me there would be no funeral, just a memorial service soon. I was not so keen on interviewing a grieving widow, and if she didn't want to speak with me, I'd respect that.

Rancho Park was a few minutes away from my office. I turned onto the street behind the Westside Pavilion and parked in front of the Ferris house. It was a small, pleasant-looking home, painted an off-white with dark green trim. A jacaranda tree stood in the front yard, its branches still bare. Even in L.A., with its mildest of winters, the leaves didn't grow back until well into April.

I knocked on the door and Hector's wife answered. She was a slender woman, close to 50, probably Hispanic, with black hair falling down past her shoulders. She had sunken eyes and wore a pale expression, not surprising, following a traumatic event.

"May I help you?"

"Mrs. Ferris," I said, handing her my card. "My name is Burnside. I used to work with Hector. A long time ago, down at the Broadway Division."

"Oh. I'm Inez. I don't think he ever mentioned you."

"Ah, yes. It was a big precinct. And I've left the LAPD."

"As did Hector," she said, opening the door. "Would you like to come in?"

I walked inside. It was a modest home but nicely furnished. The entryway led into a small living room with the kitchen off to one side. Through the window I saw a few people sitting on plastic lawn chairs on a patio, talking quietly. In the living room, an entire wall was plastered with photos and commendations, many showing Hector in uniform, along with various certificates of achievement. In one photo was a shot of the two of them on their wedding day. A few children's pictures were scattered about.

"First, I want to express my condolences about Hector. Tragic. It was a horrible thing. I'm sorry for your loss."

"Thank you," Inez said. "Yes, it was horrible. I've spoken with the homicide detectives. They promised they would find out who did this. I hope they do. For Hector's soul to rest in peace. For closure."

"Yes," I replied. "And that's part of why I'm here. I met with Hector the day before this happened. I'm a Private Investigator now. I was working on something with BMB. I'm wondering if Hector talked about what he did there."

"Some, I guess."

"Do you think what happened to Hector might have had something to do with his work at BMB?"

"I don't know. One of the detectives was thinking it might have been someone Hector had collared years ago. Maybe someone who had gotten out of jail and wanted vengeance."

"That's possible," I said. "And I'm sure they're looking at who may have been released recently. But did Hector ever mention a person named Eric Starr?"

Inez thought for a moment. "I don't believe so."

"Hmmm," I thought. That removed a big reason explaining why I was here. Then I recalled something. "What about Patty Muckenthaler?"

Her eyes narrowed. "Oh, yes. A number of times. It seemed like she was creating problems."

"In what way?"

"Hector said she would get people fired just because she didn't like them. Or to help her career. To make more money. She would say or do anything. Hector thought that woman was dangerous."

This comment was a little odd, given that Hector had the same reputation at the Broadway division. Perhaps it took one to know one. "Did he mention anything specific Patty was doing? Any particular case he was working on with her?"

"Well, apparently some people at BMB were engaging in, ah, inappropriate behavior. Patty would complain, Hector would investigate, and then the people would get fired. After a while, Hector told me he thought Patty might be making stories up. Just to get rid of people."

"Why do you say that?"

"Because Patty would get promoted or take over their work after they left. Things always panned out very well for her. Hector did not trust Patty."

"Did you tell this to the detectives?"

"No, they didn't ask. And I honestly didn't think of it until now. Until you asked specifically about Patty. Hector never mentioned a problem with anyone at work. I talked to the detectives again, a few days after Hector was ... was killed," she said, her voice choking. "I couldn't speak about things with anyone right away. It hurt too much. It was too much of a shock."

"I understand."

"As I said, the detectives were more focused on people Hector had put away while he was on the job. And also about other officers in the LAPD. Ones who might have had a resentment."

"A grudge?"

"Hector did not tolerate poor behavior among his officers. He was a Lieutenant. He took his job seriously and he felt not all the officers did. That might have been his Achilles' heel. He reported some of them. Naturally those officers disliked him. One of the other detectives I spoke with thought it could have been another police officer."

I had been considering this. It was not an implausible theory, and I thought back to my interview the other night with Hector's beer-swilling neighbor. Hector had been out of the LAPD for a couple of years. People do hold grudges, but normally not this long. And it would often take a more recent incident to set them off. Revenge might be a dish best served cold, but not this cold. And a cop, someone well versed in criminal behavior, was unlikely to take someone out in such a gruesome manner, one where the chances of getting caught were exponentially high. Whoever did this had to have been very angry, unhinged at the very least, and wanted Hector Ferris to suffer. It might have been a cop, but I was having serious doubts.

"Any other names of people from BMB you can think of? Not necessarily people you think could have done this, but maybe those who might know something?"

Inez shook her head. "I'm afraid not. Again, Hector didn't speak about many people there, Patty was the exception. I can't even imagine who would do something this heinous. No matter what the issue."

To that I agreed. I thanked her again for her time and apologized for the intrusion. Once outside, I climbed into my Pathfinder. The BMB Tower was only a few minutes away, but it was getting close to lunch and I sensed I wouldn't find Patty Muckenthaler at her desk now. As I considered how I'd go about approaching her again, my phone rang. It was Roberto.

"Burnside. Listen, I'm here at the Malomar Hotel near Westwood. I figured you'd want to know about this before it hits the news. I also need to speak with you about it."

"What's that?"

"Homicide. We think it happened sometime last night, maybe in the early evening. Housekeeping found him this morning. Jay Strong. Used to coach over at SC, we talked about him the other day. Someone shot him to death. Multiple gunshot wounds. Close range, looks like there was a struggle."

Twelve

The Malomar Hotel sat along the Wilshire Corridor, an area teeming with one beautiful high-rise condo after another. Driving eastbound, this was a two-mile artery that connected Westwood and Beverly Hills. It was mostly residential, with the occasional hotel or upscale senior citizen residence tucked in. The Malomar's entrance was fronted by a semicircular driveway for valet parking, and a number of flags flew near the front door, trumpeting the hotel's corporate parent.

I used the valet, for no other reason than restricted parking in the neighborhood often made it difficult to find a space nearby. Local residents had long ago declared war on visitors who dared to park in spaces on their streets. For people living near shops and restaurants, this was actually a legitimate issue. For people living in less trafficked areas, the reasons were less than noble. Often, residents simply wanted to use their garages for storage and didn't want to park down the street if an itinerant guest claimed the one space in front of their home.

The Malomar was a boutique hotel and that meant cool furnishings and small rooms. The lobby was beautiful, with an series of gold chandeliers providing indirect lighting. There were some comfy chairs sprinkled about, and a Persian rug covered much of the dark wood floor. A few blue-and-green striped glass vases were filled with fresh cut flowers. Colorful paintings hung on the walls. The decor was heightened sophistication, elegant without trying to be.

I strolled through the lobby, past a number of uniformed police officers. When I reached the elevator, a dour-looking man in a sharp blue blazer and pinkish tie inquired if I was a guest at the hotel. I countered by asking if he was with the police.

"No, I'm the assistant manager of the hotel," he said. "And you?"

"I'm here on official business."

"And what business is that, sir?" he asked.

"The business of trying to figure out why someone was shot to death in your hotel."

He looked askance at my comment. I flashed my fake gold shield at him and crisply directed him to kindly step aside. Not entirely sure of what to make of this, and not wanting to cause a scene, he moved back. I walked into the elevator and pushed the button that said six. He was still looking quizzically at me as the elevator door closed. I never saw him again.

Room 644 was at the end of the hall, and it wasn't hard to find. There were people going in and out of the room, with half a dozen uniforms, a few plainclothes officers and a number of people from the Coroner's office moving languidly about. Glancing inside, I saw a lamp had been knocked over, a glass coffee table shattered, and dark red blood stains were evident on both the blanket and sheets. A detective wearing a legitimate gold shield asked what I wanted, and I told him Sergeant De Santos had sent for me. He told me to wait down the hall. A few minutes later, Roberto approached.

"Burnside. Thanks for coming."

"Sure. What do you know so far?"

"As far as we can tell, the room was rented by Jay. Reservation was in his name for two nights. The problem is the desk clerk distinctly remembers a woman checking in, using Jay's credit card."

"That didn't arouse any suspicion?"

"Jay could be a woman's name, I guess. Not every hotel requires ID when someone checks in. We're running the credit card number to see if it had been stolen and used elsewhere recently."

"What did the desk clerk say the woman looked like?" I asked.

"Blonde, late thirties, attractive," Roberto said, eyeing me carefully. "Sound like anyone you might know?"

"Sounds like half the women on the Westside," I muttered, before providing Roberto with what he was looking for. "I've only met her once or twice, but it could have been Kitty. Jay's wife."

"Okay. That's one reason why I wanted to talk to you. You knew Jay pretty well, so I figured you might know the spouse. I sent a detective over to their apartment in Brentwood. She might not have done it, so we have to inform her of what happened. But you know as well as I do, the spouse is the first suspect. And those domestic disturbances are making it look obvious. But you never know. They'll bring the wife over to the station for questioning."

"Any idea about time of death?"

"The maid found him this morning, we think it probably happened last night, *rigor mortis* had already started to set in. But no one around here heard a thing. We already found shell casings, looks like a .357 was the murder weapon. I'm sure he was dead right away, that's a gun that means business. Say, let me ask you something."

"What's that?"

"When you stopped by the station earlier this week, Jay's name came up. When's the last time you saw him? You said you had lunch with him that day. Seen him since?"

I took a breath "Yeah. On campus."

"And?"

I looked down at the hallway floor. It had thick carpeting, charcoal gray, with geometric patterns to it. There was a side table nearby with a beautiful glazed pot sitting on it. I'll say this for the Malomar. They didn't cut corners. Everything here was first rate.

"Jay was troubled," I said. "Marital problems. He was convinced his wife was having an affair. Thought it was with someone at BMB. He didn't know who, but the whole thing was consuming him."

"So that leaves us with two likely suspects. The wife or her lover. Maybe both."

"Or maybe some girl Jay was having a fling with. Unlikely, but possible."

"True. That might explain the credit card. He could have handed it to her and told her to check in."

"Maybe," I sighed. "You guys find anything in the room?"

Roberto said they had. "They're dusting it for prints, but in a hotel room that won't give us much. Jay had some scratches on his face, so it looks like there was a scuffle. We'll see if any DNA turns up, but I'm not counting on much there. If it wasn't the wife, the other party would need to be in the system."

"Probably not," I mused. "Unless he was with a pro."

"Yeah," he said, and then one of the detectives approached us. He was a well-built man in his 30s, wearing a blue windbreaker with LAPD on the back. He had latex gloves on and was holding something in his hand.

"Hey, Sarge," he called, holding up a watch. "Check this out. Might have been left behind by another guest, but I don't think so, maid would have found it. We discovered it under the bed, could have come off during a struggle. Guess someone here wasn't hurting for money."

The watch was a Rolex, gold face with a silver-and-gold band. I took a closer look at it, keeping my face within a few inches of the watch for more than a few seconds, studying it carefully.

"Nope," I said. "It's a knockoff."

Roberto looked at me. "How can you tell?"

"Check out the second hand. It moves every second and then stops. A real Rolex has a sweeping motion. There's no date magnifier, either. They're expensive, so knockoffs don't have them. And listen to it. This one makes a ticking sound. You don't get that with a Rolex."

"Pretty impressive, Burnside," Roberto said, looking at me oddly. "You have a side business fencing stolen jewelry?"

"I like trivia," I shrugged.

"Interesting," he said. "But I'll bet there are a lot of fake Rolex watches around."

"Maybe so. From what I've heard, everyone at BMB got one for Christmas last year."

*

The police would be speaking today with Kitty Strong, her boss Patty Muckenthaler, and maybe even her brother-in-law, Nick Roche. I would talk to them soon enough, but today wouldn't be that day. Running into detectives at the BMB headquarters would be awkward to say the least. But there was someone connected to BMB who could answer some questions for me. He just might need a little prodding.

I found a spot along Figueroa Avenue, down the street from a cluster of fast food joints, and catty-cornered to the USC campus. I stopped and ordered a turkey sub for lunch, eating it while I absently scanned my phone for news. Nothing about Jay Strong. Not yet. Driving onto campus, I lucked out and grabbed an open parking space on the first level of the structure, closest to the Cinema school.

Lucas Kanter's door was closed, but I heard voices inside, the kind of playful, laughing voices bespeaking a party to which only two people had been invited. I sat outside and listened to the overt flirting, realizing it could also have been the rehearsal of a scene from a play or movie. Finally the door opened, and an attractive coed with long, straight blonde hair and a giddy smile emerged. She turned back to thank the professor for his help, and he reminded her to file her internship application before the end of the month.

"Hello, Doctor," I said, walking into the office. "Sorry I don't have an appointment."

"Oh," Kanter said, a bit startled. "I didn't know you'd be here, Burnside."

"It's a day of surprises. A week of them, in fact. Thank God it's Friday."

"Uh, yes. You know, I do have a class to teach soon," he pointed out, which might explain why he didn't ask me to sit down. "What's up?"

"You've heard someone tried to kill me in the Laputa parking lot the other day?"

He stared at me. "I heard about an incident there ... I had no idea you were involved."

"Yeah. Lucky for me I was a better shot."

"My goodness," he said, blinking a few times. "That's terrible. Who was it?"

"Apparently another private investigator. Someone with a connection to BMB. Name's Mike Black. There was an empty file in his office. Any ideas who at BMB might have hired him?"

"Of course not," he said. "I know the company hires investigators upon occasion. We did hire you of course. But that usually falls under Hector's domain. Or did, I suppose."

"Yes. But Hector wasn't the one who hired me. Nick

Roche did. Might he have been the one to have hired this particular P.I.?"

Kanter shook his head in disbelief. "You'd have to ask him. I have no idea. But I couldn't imagine why. This doesn't add up. We just hired you to look into Eric Starr. That was Nick's call. And Jay Strong was the one who recommended you to him."

"What stake do you have in all this?" I asked, flinching at the sound of Jay's name.

"What do you mean?"

"First, tell me what you know about Jay."

"Jay? Last year he found out I was on the board at BMB, and he was railing about the place. About how someone needs to look into what's really going on there. The place is a cesspool, yada, yada. I don't know what he thought was going on there. But I suppose he pushed Nick to bring you in."

"How about you? I mean, would you have any reason to want to dig up dirt on Eric Starr?"

"That's preposterous," he sniffed. "I can't imagine why you'd ask."

"I'm asking everybody. At this point, no one is off limits."

"Well, I have no reason to dig up dirt on anyone," he insisted.

"And Patty? What's her role here?"

"You're insane. You know, you're starting to get on my nerves. You can't just barge in ... "

At this point, I grabbed Lucas Kanter by the front of his shirt. I was tired of getting the run-around, tired of doing an investigation where no one wanted to cooperate, and especially tired of dead bodies. I didn't like getting shot at, and I had an outsized concern that might happen once again. And after seeing the remains of Jay Strong in a Westwood hotel room, I was tired of playing nice. I didn't have much to lose at this point.

I shoved Kanter up against a bookcase and put my face close to his. He tried to wiggle out of my grasp, but that made me just grab hold of him tighter. His breathing grew rapid and his mouth began to curl in fear.

"I want some answers here," I growled. "I want to know why I was really brought in on this case and why someone wants me out of the way."

"Good Lord," he whimpered. "Okay. It's not what you think."

I relaxed my grip. Just a bit. "Go on."

"There are some internal candidates for CEO. Patty's one of them. She's been threatening the board to go public with a multimillion-dollar lawsuit if she doesn't get the job. She won't get it, but she can cause a lot of headaches. There's been repeated harassment charges. But half the board was intent on hiring someone from the outside, and Eric was the someone they wanted. So we're just trying to confirm things before we finalize the deal."

"Then why set me up?" I demanded. "Who was involved in getting me to go to Laputa the other day?"

"That wasn't us. Honest. I don't know who was behind that. This corporate shit can get intense. There's a lot of money at stake here."

I took my hands off of him and stepped back. This was

only partially making sense. And it didn't explain why anyone needed to get run over, kidnapped or shot to death.

"Is Patty crazy enough to murder anyone? Or pay to have them murdered?"

Kanter straightened his clothes out and regained some composure. "My goodness, but you're an excitable guy. Before all this I would have said no. Now I'm not so sure. On the one hand, it's only just a job. On the other hand, the CEO position pays a ton of money and some people will do crazy things to get their hands on it."

I had spent many years trying to understand criminal behavior, and had learned some lessons. I felt I understood why people stole: they were either desperate or they grew up in a subculture where this was considered acceptable. I knew why many people sold drugs: they sometimes saw this as their only way out of a life of poverty. I had an understanding of why people killed in the heat of the moment: their emotions reached a boiling point at which they could no longer control them. But the blind pursuit of money was not something I could ever fully grasp. Having a family now, I understood the importance of taking care of loved ones and making them comfortable. But in the end, you still have to be able to look at yourself in the mirror.

I considered Kanter. I didn't think he was involved in anything underhanded here, and I began to feel a little badly about assaulting him. Only a little, mind you. Getting shot at was still toying with my nerves and affecting my behavior in an adverse way. This wasn't how

I normally operated and I didn't like thinking of myself as a roguish thug. I had had some prior experience with post-traumatic stress disorder and had a funny feeling I might be afflicted again.

"Where can I find Patty?" I finally asked. "And I'd like you to get me in to see her. Without letting her know I'm coming."

"If that'll get you out of here quicker, then let me make a call," he said and picked up the desk phone, his hands trembling slightly. He punched in a number, talked for a few minutes and wrote something down on a slip of paper. "Take this. I just spoke with someone in the IT department. I had them look at Patty's schedule in Outlook. She's on location tomorrow, but it's just next to Playa Vista. In the Ballona Wetlands. She's supposed to be at the shoot most of the day."

"All right," I said and then pointed my index finger at him and gave him a warning. "Again, don't give Patty a head's up I'm coming."

"Trust me, I'm not here to help Patty. Her act has gotten stale. This isn't the first time she's threatened BMB. In the past, we've capitulated. But even if something bad comes up on Eric Starr, I can't see her being the one to take the reins."

"At this point, I could care less who takes over BMB. I've got bigger concerns. Like staying alive."

"Wait a minute. I don't understand something," he said. "Isn't it the job of the police to look into capital crimes? Why are you looking into Hector's murder?"

"How have the police been doing so far?" I snapped. "I

was brought into this to do a background check and look what it's turned into. Hector got run down and someone almost killed me the other day. That changes my involvement. And there's something else I didn't tell you. There's been another murder. I just found out this morning. I'm surprised you haven't been notified."

"My God. Who now?"

"I'll let the police fill you in on that."

Kanter checked his cell phone. "I have a number of messages," he said, and he began listening to them. I thought of leaving, but I wanted to see the look on his face when he heard about Jay. I saw his eyes widen as he listened to one of the messages and his mouth opened. He put down the phone and looked at me.

"I had no idea there'd been more of this."

"Now you know."

"Why would she have done this?" he said, looking dazed.

I peered at him. "Why would *she* have done *what*?"

"Kitty Strong," he said, his voice choked with emotion. "They just ... they found her body. In her apartment. In Brentwood. They found her slumped in a chair ... with a gun in her hand."

Thirteen

Roberto left a message for me about Kitty Strong as well, his voice sounding tense and a little dry, but he told me there was no need to come by again. That was fine by me. I had witnessed enough crime scenes for the day. And for the week. I was tired and weary and I had no desire to conduct any more business today. Four people were dead, all had ties to BMB, and yet the pieces to the puzzle remained scattered. Roberto told me that while the obvious scenario was Kitty Strong had committed suicide, there were also growing doubts.

I relieved Carla at about 3:00 pm and spent the rest of the afternoon playing with Marcus in the backyard. I worked with him on how to catch a Nerf football, although I don't think he fully understood the concept of "looking" the ball into his hands. He dropped it more times than he caught it. But when he did make a catch, I gave him a hearty round of applause as a reward. And like a real receiver, he jumped up and down to celebrate every time he caught the ball.

Next, we played balloon tap, which was a game of seeing how many times we could tap a two-day old red balloon back and forth without it ever touching the ground. After a few miscues, we got the hang of it, but then Marcus hit it a little too well, causing the balloon to rise and get caught in a tree limb. I finally dislodged it by tossing a stick up into the tree, but while the balloon floated down, the stick was now caught in the branch. Marcus insisted we "save" the stick, and after some futile attempts at knocking it down with a different stick, I finally pulled out a stepladder and retrieved it, coming dangerously close to tumbling off the ladder in the process. The irony of almost getting seriously injured retrieving an errant stick, two days after someone fired a gun in my direction was not lost on me.

Gail came home, and since it had been a long week for both of us, we decided Friday night was a good night to order pizza. After dinner, Marcus settled in to watching cartoons and I lumbered off into the den to sink into an easy chair and let my mind wander aimlessly. Gail walked in a little while later and sat on the armrest next to me.

"Penny for your thoughts?"

"Make it a nickel," I said. "The price of everything is going up."

"I hope you're not worrying about money. We're doing okay."

"Not worrying. Just thinking about it."

"Something to do with the case you're working on?" she asked.

"Indeed. I got some more bad news today."

"You mean Jay and Kitty Strong?"

"You heard?"

"It was all over the news. I'm sorry. I remember meeting them once. Some coaches dinner at Johnny's house in Palos Verdes."

"Jay was the one responsible for getting me the gig with BMB," I told her. "We had lunch this week. I also dropped by his office the next day. He didn't sound happy at all. His marriage was falling apart and he was clearly in pain."

"Do you think it was really a murder-suicide? That's what's being reported."

"No. That just doesn't hold water. It sounds like Kitty rented the hotel room for a tryst. Jay might have tracked her to the room and confronted the pair. But that's where things don't line up. How would Kitty get a gun? Why would she shoot Jay? Would she really have been so remorseful that she'd go back and end it all?

"And most importantly, who was she with?" Gail pondered, as she descended softly into my lap.

"Yes," I said and put my arm around her and stroked her hair. "There's another party to this mess. Once they're found, then maybe, just maybe, all the other pieces will come together. Who killed Hector Ferris? Who was behind the plan to abduct me?"

"Oh," she said. "I think you heard, but on that subject, the police officially absolved you. They've concluded your actions were taken in self-defense. No charges are going to be filed against you."

"Thank you," I said, reaching over and kissing her cheek. "For everything."

"You're welcome. By the way, how are things going with the background check on Eric Starr? The thing BMB actually hired you to do?"

"I've found out a few things. He was briefly taken into custody for assaulting the wife of his former business partner, Jack Beale. Happened shortly after Beale was killed in the boating accident. Not sure who threw the first punch, but when there's a lot of money at stake, things can often get nasty."

"You had mentioned Eric Starr earlier in the week. I actually found out some interesting scuttlebutt on Laputa."

"My, but you're a veritable gold mine of information today. I should be paying you part of my fee from BMB. That is if they pay me. I haven't submitted my invoice to Nick Roche yet, but I'm going to bill him for more than we estimated."

"Oh, I'm sure they'll pay you. In fact, tell them your wife is an Assistant City Attorney. I'll bet they expedite your check."

"I may do that. But tell me more about Laputa."

"Yes. But you need to be very careful with this. It can't be made public unless you've uncovered a felony. You have to give me your word."

"All right," I said.

"The boating accident. You know that Jack Beale's body was never found. But an employee who was on the boat had made a comment to one of the investigators. They saw someone swimming at one point. Out in the middle of the ocean. But they couldn't be sure. They said they were pretty tipsy."

"Not a surprise. The whole company seems like it's one big party. But did this witness personally see Jack go overboard?"

"No. But they swore they saw somebody swimming. The waves were choppy."

"And they didn't think to call out or get someone's attention?" I asked.

"No. And their story is iffy, because most of all, they were intoxicated. They thought the person was swimming with purpose. Swimming away, not in distress at all. And toward another boat nearby."

"And that bit of information remained private."

"It did," she said. "I'm not sure why, but it's sealed. And if I want to keep myself in the good graces of the City Attorney, it needs to remain that way. And I'm not sure any crime was actually committed. But like I said, if you uncover a felony, all bets are off. I'm not protecting a murderer just for the sake of office politics."

"Did this employee have a name?"

"Yes, indeed," Gail said, looking me straight in the eye. "And it explains how she came to know my boss, Steve Reinhart. The witness was Anna Faust."

*

The next day was Saturday, which meant most people wouldn't be working. Except for me. I woke up at my customary 5:00 a.m., the first Gulfstream jets shaking me awake as they departed from Santa Monica Airport. I rolled out of bed and took a short walk to my desk. After doing a brief scan of the news, I decided to see if I could track down Jack Beale's former girlfriend, Wanda, on the Internet. She was a small piece to this puzzle, but a piece nonetheless. Finding her wasn't as difficult as I thought it might be.

Marcus had inherited my habit of being an early riser, and he climbed into my lap to watch what I was doing on the computer. After reminding me of my promise to take him out for a waffle dinner, I told him I would deliver soon. In the interim, I got up and made him scrambled eggs, and then we went into his room, where I showed him how to make a paper airplane. Chewy wandered in by this time and proceeded to jump up and grab every plane we launched out of the air with her teeth, and then darted into another room to deposit them one by one. By the time we were done, the living room was scattered with downed aircraft.

After Gail woke up, I made a quick phone call to ensure my first appointment was still at home, and then hung up quickly when the person answered. I left the house around 10:00 am and drove up to the Valley. Chucky Flange lived in what was once a decent, middle-class apartment complex along Sherman Way in Van Nuys. That was many years ago. Now there was bright red graffiti scrawled along the side of the building, and a few windows were broken. Trash spilled out of a dumpster next to the parking garage. At one point there might have been a working security door, but that was probably quite some time ago. A couple of empty brown beer bottles were laying on the ground.

I yanked the front door open, walked inside and climbed up a flight of uneven stairs before I found apartment 2F and rapped softly. Then I rapped a little harder, and finally I began to pound my fist. It took a minute, but I did hear stirring in the apartment.

Eventually, a few footsteps were audible and a sleepy voice came through the door.

"Yeah?"

"UPS," I said. "Got a package."

"Uh, just leave it by the door."

"Got to sign for it. Only take a second."

I heard the sound of two deadbolts snapping and then the door opened. I lowered my shoulder and barreled into the apartment. Chucky Flange was in no position to stop me. And unless he was keeping a pistol in his boxers, it was pretty clear he was unarmed.

"Hey, what the hell?!" he demanded, scooting back.

"Let's just say our last meeting was insufficient."

"Hey, man. I got a gun here."

"Chucky. Look at me. Remember who I am?"

He blinked. "Yeah."

"So you know if you pull a gun on me, there's a good chance you'll be dead in two seconds. Just like Mike Black."

"Who?"

"Mike Black," I repeated a little testier. "The guy you tried to help in the kidnapping job the other day. At Laputa. The reason the police detained you. You do recall that, right?"

He nodded and swallowed.

"Look," I said, "we can do this the easy way and it won't take long. Or we can do it the hard way and you'll end up putting an ice pack on your face. At the very least."

He thought about this some more before he finally walked over and sat down on a black vinyl-covered kitchen chair. I took that as an invitation to sit down, too. He was a big man, barrel-chested but with some ripples of fat around his gut, and a wide slab of flesh for a face. He had a small mouth and small black eyes. I sat across from him and put my hands on the table.

"Do you know what I want from you?" I asked.

"Uh-uh."

I looked down at his kitchen table. There was a brass ash tray loaded with cigarette butts, a few empty cans of Bud Lite, and a roll of nickels. I had a funny feeling they were there for a specific purpose. When someone wraps their fist around a roll of coins, the hand becomes tighter and less susceptible to an injury, yet their punches can still do considerable damage.

"You usually carry around a roll of nickels?" I asked.

"When I need to," he shrugged.

"Most people use a roll of quarters."

"Nickels are cheaper."

"Okay, Chucky. Keep your hands away from the table. And let me explain how this is going to work. Tell me about Mike Black. I want everything. If you're forthcoming, this is the last time you'll ever see me. If not, I'll have you back in LAPD custody. After I mess up your face. No amount of nickels is going to help you. And you know I can deliver on that promise, too."

Frankly, given Chucky Flange's bulk, I wasn't entirely certain I could deliver. And I was quite sure that the LAPD was done with him. But hefty threats carry with them the appearance of being real, and they have a remarkable way of getting tongues wagging. Chucky Flange began to talk.

He told me some of what I already knew. That he met Mike Black at the gym, had assisted him a few times, usually doing nothing more strenuous than to look menacing. And that Mike Black called him on Wednesday, wanting his help in handling a situation. He needed Chucky around to help pick someone up at Laputa.

"What did he plan to do to me?"

"He said he needed to send you a message, teach you a lesson. I don't know, something like that. You were causing problems for his client," he shrugged, holding up his palms. "He told me we'd collect you, drive you to this vacant warehouse in Reseda, tie you up and smack you around a bit. Nothing serious. Just get you scared off. He said it would be fun."

"Smack me around," I repeated. "That your idea of fun?"

"Hey, I didn't think about it too much, okay? He said he'd pay me $1,000. For half a day's work. I do construction and business is up and down. When you need money, you don't question things."

"Go on."

"Yeah, right. He said we'd pick you up in the Laputa garage, load you into the van and take off. I didn't expect things to get crazy."

"Who was behind all this? Who was the client?"

"He didn't give a name. Just that they were high up in the entertainment industry. A real heavy hitter, some big-shot executive. Mike thought we might get more work from them. Maybe even get cast in a movie. I think he mentioned BMB. Something to do with production."

David Chill

Fourteen

The freeways were typically wide open on a Saturday, and today was no different. The drive from Van Nuys down to Playa Vista took 20 minutes. Decades ago, the Marina Freeway had been called the Richard M. Nixon Freeway. That was in the early 1970s. It was a short-lived nomenclature that was hastily changed after Nixon resigned from office. For years, it was simply referred to as the 90 Freeway, but eventually it was renamed after nearby Marina del Rey.

I turned left on Culver and drove a few minutes toward the Ballona Wetlands. This was a large, undeveloped parcel of marshland, one of the few open areas still left in Los Angeles. After a rainy winter, one could go to the Wetlands and commune with nature. The foliage would be green and lush, and the mustard plants could sprout well past six feet high. The Wetlands are also home to some exotic birds and small, mischievous wildlife. But over the past few winters, California had had little rain and the drought-stricken plants had become withered, bone-dry and gray. Whatever still lived here was not worth looking at. And the wetlands part of the name had clearly become a misnomer.

The area is normally not open to the public and an 11-mile chain link fence that surrounds the perimeter testifies to that. Even getting a permit to film there takes some doing. But it appears BMB was able to navigate the bureaucracy and greased whatever levers of power needed lubricating. A group of cars and trailers were situated in a remote patch of the Wetlands, with a number of cameras, booms and lighting fixtures set up.

I parked and walked over to where a gaggle of below-the-line crew were setting up for the next shot. A couple of actors stood nearby chatting, looking familiar, but in the same way as someone I saw every day in my office building might look familiar. I recognized them, but I couldn't place them. It reminded me of the old joke that in L.A. sometimes the guy standing behind you in the Starbucks line with his baseball cap pulled down low, and a three-day beard growth and a vague resemblance to George Clooney actually *was* George Clooney. I wandered around the set, looking at faces, casually nodding and smiling. If you acted like you belonged, most people had better things to do than question why you were there. After a couple of minutes of strolling, a familiar sight came into view. Naturally she was on her phone.

I walked up to Patty Muckenthaler and waved my hand to get her attention. She responded by rolling her eyes, mouthing an obscenity and turning her back to me. In a typical situation, I might have given her a few minutes to finish her call. But that insult, coupled with the strong likelihood she might never be finished with her calls, at least not until the director asked for quiet on the set, propelled me to move things along.

In the world of criminal law, the simple act of touching someone can be considered assault. It is also very intrusive. In the world of the entertainment industry, touching someone's phone can be taken as a deep sign of disrespect. With little to lose, I walked up to Patty. Her back was still turned to me, so I reached over, grabbed her phone and ripped it out of her hand.

"She'll call you back," I said into the speaker and hung up.

"What the hell do you think you're doing?!" she screamed.

"Getting your attention. I think I achieved that."

"Give me my phone back!"

"After we finish our conversation, I'll be happy to."

"We don't have anything more to talk about," Patty snarled. "In fact, I think you said plenty the other day."

"And I think you haven't said enough. Not anywhere near enough."

"Like what?" she demanded. "Do you want to grill me some more about Hector Ferris? You really think I have time to run someone over?"

"No, Lucas Kanter tells me your calendar is quite full," I said, watching carefully to see her react to the name of a key board member.

"Lucas Kanter?" she asked, slowing down and showing some genuine curiosity. "What are you talking to him about?"

"We talked about some of your schemes to get ahead. How to climb the corporate ladder by getting rid of everyone ahead of you."

Patty stared at me. "Just what do you think you know about me?"

"I know how you've gotten your last few promotions. Threatening lawsuits, charging sexual harassment. Nice way to define your career. But I also know that four people are dead this week and they all connect back to BMB. And maybe to you."

"Are you nuts? You think I'm actually involved in killing four people? To get ahead?"

"I don't like to think so. But I've been involved in a nasty trail of human carnage this week. Someone committed these acts. I don't know if it was you. I just need to figure out why you'd stoop to murder. I don't like to think career ambition could lead to this. But then again, this is show biz."

"I didn't do anything," she insisted.

"How do you explain Jay Strong?"

"Jay? What'd you think, I'd tangle with a guy twice my size, wrestle with him and then shoot him? Are you mad?"

"How do you know someone was wrestling with him?" I asked.

"Because that's what the police told me, you idiot. I couldn't believe they would question me about Jay. And then Kitty? They're saying her death was made out to be a suicide, but they think someone shot her, too."

"Who was Kitty having an affair with?"

"What?" she asked, blinking her eyes.

"Don't play dumb. She worked for you. You had to have known she and Jay were having marital problems."

Patty looked away and thought for a moment. A few members of the crew had apparently seen us having an intense discussion and had wandered over. Patty shooed them away.

"Kitty and I were friends. Yes, I knew she was having problems in her marriage. But I don't exactly follow everyone around. I may have used some leverage to advance my career. Lucas and his big mouth. But that doesn't mean I killed anyone."

"Who's job were you after this time?"

"There are some things that are not your concern," she said.

"Were you the one charging third-person sexual harassment? Seeing someone at work making sexual advances and filing charges?"

Patty's mouth opened and her stare turned into a glare. "That's an ongoing legal action," she said, looking around and starting to get her bearings again. "And it's way above your pay grade. Unless you're planning to beat that out of me. I hear you're a tough guy. But there are a bunch of tough guys here."

"You mean a bunch of actors?" I sneered. "They're more concerned with getting the timbre of their voices right."

"There's a lot of crew here. You want to fight everyone on the set?"

I looked at her. There was only so much water I was going to get out of this stone. But just then I noticed something on her wrist and became curious.

"That's a nice watch. Company Christmas gift?"

Patty blinked for a moment. "As a matter of fact, it was," she said, seemingly relieved I had changed the subject.

"A Rolex, I imagine."

"Yes," she said, holding it up to show me. I eyed it carefully and was surprised at a few things. There was no ticking sound. The second hand was sweeping cleanly around the dial. And the date magnifier actually worked and made the number easier to read.

"This is a real Rolex," I said.

"Of course it's a real Rolex."

"I thought BMB gave out knockoffs to employees."

"Good Lord. I make a seven-figure income. Do you think senior executives are going to wear cheap, fake watches? Yes, most of the employees got knockoffs. The Presidents got the real deal. We don't get nickel-and-dimed at this level."

That made sense. And it sparked an idea. But I had another question that was nagging at me.

"Okay. One last question."

"Make it quick," she said impatiently.

"When I met you for breakfast this week, you acted like you hadn't heard about what happened to Hector the night before. That was play acting. A senior executive who was unaware their Security Director had been murdered the day before? Even if you hadn't been notified, it was all over the news. Why were you pretending you didn't know?"

Patty took a breath. "I had just met you. I didn't know what your role was. Nick wouldn't say and Hector wouldn't say. The timing of our meeting was strange. I thought you might have been the one who ran over Hector. And that maybe you were covering your tracks by meeting with me. And I didn't know what you had up your sleeve. I thought maybe I'd be your next victim."

As ridiculous as that sounded on the face of things, in hindsight there were strands of truth in what she said. Patty's paranoid mind might well have been in overdrive that day. Paranoia is the height of self-centered behavior, and Patty was clearly as egocentric a person as they came. The idea that I might have nothing better to do but go around and kill people was absurd. But I could also see how it might be possible for someone with the sickest of minds to come to that abhorrent conclusion. And someone had, after all, committed cold-blooded murder, dragging Hector Ferris savagely beneath the wheels of their car.

I gave Patty her phone back and said goodbye. She responded by storming off. If she mouthed an obscenity, she did so with her back turned to me. I returned to my Pathfinder and drove away, and in two minutes the barren Wetlands were nothing more than a faint blip in my rear-view mirror.

I had a funny feeling the folks at Celestial Productions would be working on Saturday. Descending into the near-empty garage beneath the Century Plaza Towers, I drove my Pathfinder slowly, stopping at each parked vehicle. With the events of the past few days still fresh in my mind, I kept one eye peeled for hidden assailants with sinister intentions. I found myself reaching into my jacket to make sure my backup .38 was still snug in its holster. The police were still hanging onto the one involved in the Mike Black shooting.

I drove along and looked at the reserved parking spaces. This being a Saturday, many of them were unoccupied, and the names of countless law firms, consulting groups and production companies were listed. Finally I came upon what I was looking for. Celestial Productions had at least a dozen parking spaces, although only two were being used today. One held a BMW 740, slotted in the space listed for Malcolm Taylor. Another held a dark green Ford Explorer, but there was no name listed, only "employee."

Pulling into a space nearby, I got out and looked at the two vehicles. The BMW looked glossy and perfect, just like any $100,000 car should look, a shiny testament to someone's success. There was something odd about the Ford Explorer, though. The hood appeared to be new, waxed to a shiny gleam. It looked better than the rest of the vehicle. I walked around the front end and saw that the bumper and the grill were brand new as well, polished chrome that looked like they had just been installed.

The lobby was empty, not surprising for a Saturday. I signed in with the sleepy guard at the desk and rode the elevator up to the 38th floor. As I walked down the hallway, it was so quiet you could hear the hum of the air conditioning. It was almost as if I had entered an isolation tank.

I opened the Celestial Productions office door quietly and walked in. The door hinges must have been well-oiled, because they made no sound whatsoever. Even pulling the handle down did not give off a discernible click. This was clearly a building where the designers ensured silence would be golden.

Adam Gee was sitting at his desk, hunched over his computer, reading something that was transfixing him. He was dressed in a gray t-shirt promoting Coachella, and also wore tan shorts and a pair of orange Nikes. In his hand was a *venti* cup from Starbucks. Judging from the steam rising upward, It looked like he had barely started in on it.

"Nothing like a pick-me-up on a lazy Saturday afternoon," I observed.

He jumped in surprise, and a bit of *latte* sloshed onto his desk. "Oh. Mr. Burnside. I wasn't expecting you."

"I prefer it that way. People don't get to prepare a script."

"Yes," he stammered. "Of course. You know, Mr. Taylor stepped out for lunch. He'll be back soon."

"Actually, I'd like to talk with you."

"Me?"

"Mmm-hmmm," I said, sitting down next to him. "Maybe start with the vehicles you drive. Then we can talk about the watches you wear."

He gave me a long, curious gaze. "I thought I told you about all of that. The watch, too. It was a company gift. And I drive a 15 year-old SUV. It belonged to an uncle of mine. He bought a new car last year and gave me his Explorer. What's this all about?"

"Hold up your wrist," I said.

He frowned and raised it. I took a good look at his watch. The sweeping second hand, the working magnifier and the silent movement told me it was real.

I spoke. "You're aware that the Security Director at BMB was murdered earlier this week."

"Yes, of course. It was all over the news," he said. "Why?"

"Where were you on Tuesday evening?"

"I was at an industry gathering that night," he said, frowning. "AFI had a function. I was there until midnight. And I have witnesses."

"Then explain how come your SUV has a brand new front end. And why you were driving a BMW when you came over to my office the other day. It's all starting to make sense now. What doesn't make any sense is why. Why would you kill Hector Ferris? And where were you the other night when Kitty Strong's husband, Jay, was shot to death at the Malomar?"

Adam gaped at me. "I ... I don't know how you could think I was involved in any of that."

"You have some explaining to do, kid," I said soberly. "Murder one carries the death penalty with it."

"I didn't murder anybody! My boss borrowed the Explorer that night."

"Oh?"

"Yeah, and he kept it all week. Said he needed to haul some things around."

Now it was my turn to gape at Adam Gee. "That might change things," I said. "In fact, that changes everything."

"Yes, indeed it does," came the smooth-as-velvet voice from behind us. I turned and saw the very handsome face of Malcolm Taylor. His broad smile was not evident, and his blue eyes weren't sparkling. He had a bandage under his chin. In his hand was a .357 Magnum.

"Didn't hear you come in," I said. "This building is awfully quiet."

"I like it that way," he said and pointed to his office. "Let's take this in there, shall we?"

Fifteen

Malcolm Taylor told Adam to wait outside. He leaned against the front of his magnificent desk. Wearing a yellow golf shirt and tan trousers, he looked dapper enough to play 18 holes at the L.A. Country Club. I sat across from him on the couch. The gun was in Taylor's right hand, aimed directly at my head. He maintained a good ten feet of separation, meaning there was no way I could lunge at him. At least not without getting shot in the process.

"You really shouldn't have been poking around in my business," Malcolm sighed with a sad shake of his head. "You should have just taken that big fat fee I offered. You would have lived a nice, full life."

"Let's just say, when I'm hired to do a job, I finish it," I responded.

"No one hired you to stick your nose into my business. Guess you never watched *Chinatown*, did you kitty-cat? Those types of people get their noses cut off. In your case, it'll be much worse."

"Don't be so hasty. You're in this mess up to your neck. It won't be long before the police add everything up. One look at Adam's SUV and they'll note something suspicious. New bumper, uneven paint job. And you took the vehicle all week, didn't you, Malcolm?"

"I did," he said, "and I'd like to see you prove anything. Where's your evidence? The sheet metal and bumper and other parts I replaced? They're all gone.

Crushed. No one'll ever find them. I hired someone off the grid. Figured the police would send an APB to every body shop in town. This way, there are no footprints."

"You stitched this together very nicely, Mr. Taylor."

"Of course. I didn't get to the top of the heap by just screwing people over. Like Patty."

I filed this tidbit away for a moment. "What about the goons you sent over to kidnap me at that garage? You're the one who sent me over there, right? Had some girl leave a message on my voice mail telling me to be at Eric Starr's office."

"Yeah, thanks for the heads up that you were looking into Laputa," Malcolm said, feeling relaxed enough to finally smile a little. "Made it convenient for me. You know, those two morons weren't supposed to shoot you. I just wanted to send you a warning. Slap you around a bit so you'd back off. You took it too seriously."

"Yeah, I do that whenever someone points a firearm at me," I said, staring at the .357 Magnum. "I'm not fond of the idea of being slapped around, either."

"You're good at what you do," he said. "I really think I could've used you as a technical advisor."

"Don't tell me you were going to make that crappy movie, *Day Watch*, or whatever it was called."

"Ha! No, again, that was a ruse, just to try and get you on my side, get you to stop looking into things. You might want to choose your words more carefully. Turns out one of your SC football players wrote it."

I frowned. "Demetrius?"

"I don't know. Something like that. Black guy from the

hood. Kanter sent it to me as a joke. I optioned it for a dollar, made the kid feel worthwhile."

"Ah, your way of giving back to the community."

"He should stick with football for now. Or something else. The world still needs people to stock shelves at Wal-Mart."

"Nice," I said dryly. "But getting back to that day at Laputa. How long do you think it will take for the police to check my phone. And find that woman who left the voice mail sending me to Laputa to get jumped?"

"Oh, good point," he said. "Thanks for reminding me. Give me your cell phone. And Burnside, don't even think about trying anything funny or I'll shoot you straight away. This isn't some cheap pistol like the one Mike Black was carrying around. Yeah, I know all about that. This one's deadly accurate. And as you mentioned, this is a mighty quiet building. Nobody will hear a thing."

I tossed my phone over to him and he slipped it into his pocket. What I didn't remind him of was that the police wouldn't need the phone to access my voice mail. Or to determine where the blocked number emanated from. Or to find the woman that left the voice mail, who almost certainly would hand over Malcolm Taylor in two seconds. When faced with being an accessory to murder, people tend to cooperate with the police.

"So tell me, Malcolm," I said, sensing Mal Taylor was the type of guy who liked to boast about his accomplishments. "Why Hector Ferris. Why kill him? And why do it so brutally? He have something on you?"

"Hector? That prick helped oust me at BMB. Pretty

clean job he did. Had me accused of sexual harassment. And I never harassed anyone. Every girl I screwed there, they wanted it. They were begging for it."

While I wasn't fully surprised at Taylor's openness, I was certainly taken aback at what he would choose to share. Malcolm Taylor's ability as a stud, and the mere thought of it made me want to puke. Why some men insisted on bragging about their sexual conquests to other men was beyond me.

"So Hector got you fired?"

"With Patty's help. They were pretty tight. They called it third-person sexual harassment. And let's just say I had a few women there. Once Patty got wind of things, she threatened to go public with it. And the board decided they didn't want the publicity, so I got packaged out."

"And you were ticked at Hector," I said. "Because Hector knew about you and Kitty Strong."

"You figured that out, huh," Malcolm said, a weird look forming in his eye. "Hector wouldn't back down, that's a problem with some of you cops. Don't understand the entertainment world. I offered him anything he could have ever wanted and he refused me. Self-righteous prick. He left me no choice. I had to take him out. And it had to hurt."

"Dragging him underneath an SUV would accomplish that," I said ruefully.

"Sure," he said. "It started out as vengeance. But to be honest, it just felt good."

"And that's why you used Adam's vehicle."

"I borrowed it. I didn't tell him about it at first, in case something unforeseen happened. He was covered, though. If anyone at the scene catches the license plate, if I need to abandon the vehicle, whatever the issue, Adam had a rock solid alibi. He was still at that AFI function. Witnesses everywhere. The SUV would have simply been reported as stolen."

"So what were you going to do about Patty? She's the one who actually filed those third-person harassment charges?"

Malcolm Taylor smiled in a manner that could only be considered cruel. "Patty? Oh, I've got plans for her. She figured that with me out of the way, she'd be elevated to CEO. What a bad move. Lucas Kanter told me there was no way that would ever happen, the board is sick of her shit. So once a new CEO gets in, Patty will be out on her ass. I've got her future all mapped out. What's left of it, that is."

"And Jay Strong? Geez, but you've had a busy week."

"Yeah," he sighed. "I didn't plan on that one happening. That was just a romantic rendezvous that went south."

"So tell me something. Why did Kitty use Jay's credit card? Wouldn't that have gotten back to him when the bill came at the end of the month?"

Malcolm shrugged. "Who knows. Their marriage was kaput, maybe this was Kitty's way of letting him know it was over. For all I know, Kitty might have even told him where we'd be. When Jay showed up, he tried to get tough with me."

"Jay's a pretty big guy," I mused. "Hard to outmuscle

someone like that."

"Yeah, well, he grabbed me and we tussled for a second or two. I finally got my handgun out and let him have it. Imagine his surprise. He thought he was going to teach me a lesson. Too bad for him, but I always pack some heat with me when I'm out on the town. L.A., you know. Lot of criminals around here."

"So I've noticed. And you set up Kitty so it would like she committed suicide."

"It was the only way out. Murder-suicide. Old story, but that got me off the hook for taking out Jay. The police are either too swamped or too lazy to dig for what really happened. So I wrapped it all up nicely for them. Even put a bow on it."

Working 13 years for the LAPD, I had met plenty of people who had come unhinged. But with most of them, you could tell just by looking at them. Their body movements, their mannerisms, their speech patterns. There was always something off. Not so with Malcolm Taylor. He was cool as ice and suave to boot, a compartmentalizing sociopath. And while his twisted mind was certainly keen, it was clear he hadn't thought out every detail.

"So how do you plan to get away with all this?" I asked.

Malcolm looked down at his gun and then at me and shrugged. "Gosh, I dunno. Can't imagine it'll be hard."

"Oh? You think because no one can hear a gunshot in this building means you're out of the woods? Just how are you going to dispose of my body? These windows don't open."

"Haven't put it all together yet. Didn't expect you here today. You're a smart guy. Tell me. What would you do in this situation? Toss your body off the roof? Or do you have a better plan?"

I stared at him. Did he really think I was going to help conjure up a scheme to murder me? But he did give me an opening. And playing along was the best chance I had right now. I tilted my head and pretended I was in deep thought. My observation of Nick Roche was now coming in handy. All I needed was a cigarette in hand to complete the image. And I actually had an idea in mind.

"Too messy," I declared. "It's not like you can pin a suicide note to my shirt. And you'd have to shoot me to get me out of here, which means blood stains on your nice rug. And your BMB connection makes you an immediate suspect, the cops know I'm looking into BMB. I mean, how many former BMB chiefs have an office in this building? The police would be looking to question you well before you could get the carpet cleaners hired."

He looked at me oddly. "Go on."

I looked back at him and noticed something. He still wore his gold bracelet, but there was no watch on his wrist. At our last meeting, his Rolex was prominently displayed on his left wrist, he removed it only to lay it down on his desk as a power move. It was strange how these things come together. Whether I could pull this off, though, was another matter.

"Wait a minute," I said. "What happened to your Rolex?"

He looked down and shrugged. "Put it down somewhere, I guess. I take it off a lot, it's probably at home. Even still, it's not like I can't afford another."

"You know, they found a Rolex on the floor at the hotel room. The Malomar. It was a BMB watch. I guess you gave them out to your employees for Christmas."

Taylor gaped at me. He clearly wasn't smiling anymore. "What are you getting at?"

"Once they run DNA testing on it, they'll find a hair or fiber on it that will link you to the murder scene. They'll know you were in the room and you killed Jay. The police have the watch. I'm sure someone, somewhere knows you own a .357. There's nothing you can do about it. Unless you have a fall guy. A sap. A foil who can take the blame for you."

"Such as?" he asked warily.

I motioned to the door. "Your assistant. Adam Gee."

"Don't be ridiculous. Adam's like a son to me."

"It's your only way out. You need to give the police someone or they'll collar you. Bring him in here. I'll lay it all out for you."

He paused for a long moment, thought about this and then punched an intercom button and told Adam to come in. The door opened a few seconds later and Adam Gee entered, looking nervous, the steaming cup of coffee in his hands starting to shake. His breathing was deep. Even Malcolm Taylor noticed it.

"What's the matter, Adam?" he asked.

"Tell him, Adam," I prodded. "Better yet, show him your watch."

"No," he said.

"What are you talking about?" Taylor asked me, his eyes darting back and forth between me and Adam, suddenly unsure of who he should be directing the questions to, or even pointing the gun at.

"That watch they found at the scene of Jay Strong's murder. It was a Rolex, but it was a knockoff. Someone like a CEO wouldn't wear a knockoff, would he?"

"No," sniffed Taylor. "I wear the real deal."

"Show him your watch, Adam," I said. "It's the real deal. The one you stole from your boss."

"I didn't ... I didn't steal it," he stammered.

"Oh? Did you call swapping watches with him something other than stealing? The watch your boss dropped at the hotel room had to be yours. It was a knockoff. Which I'm sure the police will figure out. These things are usually numbered somewhere. The company knows who got what. And then you'll be the one the police will charge with double murder. If you're lucky you'll get life, otherwise you're looking at a lethal injection."

"What?!" Adam said, his voice rising. "Malcolm, I'm sorry I took it. You leave it lying around all the time. I swapped mine for yours for a couple of days. I wanted to show off. I just borrowed a watch, for goodness sake. I didn't murder anyone!"

I shook my head. "The funny thing is, kid, the police aren't going to care. They'll identify it as your watch that was at the murder scene, and you'll take the blame for killing Jay Strong. And they'll see it was your vehicle that ran over Hector Ferris. The police won't believe you never left that AFI gathering. They'll figure you just snuck out, took your Explorer and drove over to Hector's house. Then drove back."

"Why would I do that?" he exclaimed. "That's crazy!"

"Sure it is. But your boss won't back you up. If he did, he'd be the one going to prison for life. Or maybe worse. It's always the underlings that take the hit for the boss, not vice versa. Right, Malcolm?"

Malcolm Taylor was processing this and looked intrigued with what he was hearing. An odd expression appeared on the corner of his mouth. The idea that he might be able to squirm out of this nasty situation had to be remarkably appealing. A minute ago, it was looking like he might have to kill me and then orchestrate a tricky maneuver to dispose of my body. And have an explanation for the police, in case Adam squealed. Or maybe shoot Adam, too. Now he had options.

"Even if I were to agree to go forward with that, and pin it on Adam," Malcolm said, "I still have the problem of you to deal with. Adam I know. You, I don't."

I took a breath and knew I would now have to put on a bravo finale. My next few words were critical. I had to convince Malcolm that I was on his side. This was an act I would need to do well if I was going to emerge from this mess alive. Having spent time recruiting high school football players for USC had sharpened my selling skills. And having grown up in L.A. might help me as well. They say every man here is an actor. Now, I'd have to prove it.

"Malcolm, I'm a reasonable man. Pay me a reasonable fee and I'll shut up. I have every reason to want to help you, because that's my one way out. I'll help you pin it all on Adam. He's your only option. The police need a culprit in the Hector Ferris murder. Adam is perfect. Better than perfect. He's tailor-made to play the part."

Adam's eyes darted back and forth, and he had the wild expression of someone who just realized he had been thrown into a parallel universe. "Malcolm, this is crazy," he pleaded. "You can't seriously consider this."

Malcolm Taylor looked at Adam and then looked back at me. "What do you consider reasonable?"

My mind raced. Too low and he'd know I wasn't serious. Too high and he'd balk. I licked my lips some more. In the back of my mind, I recognized licking my lips was a tell. But it was practically involuntary. "I'll do it for a million bucks," I said. "Cash. And when I get it, I'll disappear forever. Keep Adam around, and he'll always have that leverage over you."

Malcolm rolled this over in his mind. He wasn't rejecting it outright, which was a good sign. But out of the corner of my eye, I realized Adam Gee was processing this, too. And he was the one who acted first.

It all happened so quickly. In a split second, Adam flung his steaming *venti latte* straight into Malcolm's face. Yelping in pain and blinded by the hot drink, Malcolm lowered the gun. Both Adam and I leaped at it, with Adam reaching Malcolm first and grabbing a hold of his arm. I was now debating the curious choice of who to punch in the face. This was not a decision that could be mulled over. But the choice was fairly easy in one regard. Adam's back was to me, and his face was tucked down and out of reach. Malcolm's, on the other hand, was in full view, easily accessible, and both of his hands were occupied, busy trying to maintain control of his gun.

I caught Malcolm with a solid right cross to the jaw. Coupled with the hot cup of coffee splashed in his face, he didn't have a lot of fortitude. His body crumpled, and his grip on the gun loosened. He didn't fall, rather, he slid slightly, trying awkwardly to maintain his equilibrium. His left hand grabbed at the desk in an attempt to steady himself. In so doing, Adam pulled the gun away. He was fumbling with it, trying desperately to secure it in his right hand and insert his finger onto the trigger.

The problem with a three-way fight is you never know who is going to do what. While I didn't think the world would be worse off if Adam aimed the gun at Malcolm and fired, there remained the ancillary issue of what Adam would do with me. Witnesses are a nuisance to the murderer, regardless of any extenuating circumstances. And I didn't think the young man would look kindly upon me, even though I had no intention of letting Malcolm Taylor slip out of this one, and I was in no way going to help him pin the murder on Adam. The big problem for me was, I feared, Adam didn't know that.

The chance to seize control of a situation is optimal when things are in flux. As one of my political science professors at USC once said, through chaos comes opportunity. Adam had managed to tighten his grip on the .357 when I reached him. Just as he was turning toward us, I reached over, raised my balled left fist high in the air, and slammed it down hard on his right forearm. Using a chopping motion that would please any martial arts instructor, I kept moving my arm forward, and followed through with the blow. Adam gasped in pain. The gun tumbled onto the floor and, because my arm was already swinging in a downward arc, my hand was the one closest to being able to retrieve it.

I grabbed the gun with my left hand and was about to transfer it to my right, when I saw Malcolm lunging at us out of the corner of my eye. I moved my right arm across my chest and unleashed a vicious back punch that caught him flush on the nose. There are few better places to land a blow. A punch in the nose is painful and disabling, and it's the type of hit that only an experienced combatant can shrug off. Malcolm might have been a good corporate infighter, but in this realm, he was out of his league. He spun around and dropped to one knee, raising his hand to his face. After a few seconds, his body slumped over onto the floor and he began to moan slightly as he writhed on the ground.

Stepping back a few paces, I put some distance between us. Still looking at Adam, I finally moved the gun to my right hand. I didn't think Adam would take a run at me, but if he did, I wanted enough time to point and shoot. Fortunately, he was still wincing, holding his wrist, a pained expression on his face.

"Hey Adam," I said.

"What?" he managed through clenched teeth.

"You didn't really think I was going to let you take the fall for all this, did you?"

"It sure sounded like it," he grimaced.

"Well, I wasn't. I can assure you of that. I hope you believe me."

"I don't know what to believe, man."

"Understandable," I shrugged. "Hey. Would you do me a favor? Go into Malcolm's pocket and hand me my phone? I think someone should call 911 and give Malcolm over to the cops, don't you? Might be quicker if I did that."

Sixteen

It took about 20 minutes for Roberto De Santos to walk through the door of Celestial Productions, followed by a coterie of uniformed officers. My guess is he left the Purdue Division shortly after my call. Saturday afternoon traffic along Olympic Boulevard was almost always light.

"Glad you're working the weekend shift," I remarked as the uniforms handcuffed both Malcolm and Adam. "Otherwise I might have to endure getting hauled in twice in one week."

"Juan usually takes Saturdays off, so I cover for him," he said. "He likes to watch the college basketball tournament. March Madness and all that."

"Glad one of you is around to lend a helping hand."

I took Roberto through the details of the past few days. While Malcolm had admitted to the murders of Hector, Jay and Kitty, the only evidence was my word and Adam's. Ballistics would comb through Adam's Ford Explorer, and I thought it was likely they'd find DNA evidence confirming Malcolm's presence behind the wheel. It wasn't solid proof, but it might be enough for the police to secure a confession. And there would surely be Malcolm's DNA on the watch he left behind in the hotel room. And perhaps even video evidence from the hotel's surveillance system in the lobby. A suspect, faced with life imprisonment at the very least, might come clean, regardless of whether he possessed a guilty conscience.

"Still leaves us with the issue of Adam Gee's involvement," Roberto mused.

"My own sense is he was probably a bystander in all this," I said. "He had no motive to kill anyone. But accessory to murder is still an option. If he turns state's evidence against Taylor, you can cut him a deal."

"Given what he's facing, I think he'll cooperate with us."

"Funny how things work out," I said, "Adam basically admitted to grand larceny when he said he took Malcolm's Rolex. That would remove him from the crime scene. Unless you were to buy into Malcolm's lame story, that Adam didn't steal the watch, but lost it when he shot Jay in the hotel room. So Adam won't even have to face charges of grand larceny for stealing a $10,000 piece of jewelry."

Roberto shook his head. "Show biz. Who needs it."

"Pays well."

"Yeah. I know it's a crazy business, but I never figured it would be this dangerous. Say, let me ask you something. We were talking about Eric Starr and Laputa earlier. Cold case. Ten people on board the yacht, and no one saw anything. You learn anything more there?"

"Well, I think Eric's partner, Jack Beale, didn't exactly fall off his yacht and into the ocean. Proving it is another matter, but I'm not so sure there's a guilty party here. We won't be getting a confession. I still need to poke around a little more."

"Okay. Keep me in the loop."

"Sure."

"Hey, one more thing," he said, holding up a finger. "I did you a solid yesterday."

"How so?"

"That warrant that was out for you, the one down in Orange County? I called Irvine P.D. Had it quashed."

I raised my eyebrows. "They were okay with that?"

"Told them you were an ex-cop. Let things get a little out of hand. They got it. When push comes to shove, most police departments will side with an ex-cop over some deputy dog working for a security patrol. And given the amount of stress you've been under this week, I figured you deserved a break."

Stress indeed. The last thing I needed to do was spend another half-day sitting inside a police station, explaining my lack of adequate respect for others and my willingness to settle verbal disputes through physical altercation. But I recognized I also needed to take stock of my actions, even if that meant trying to prevent future events from devolving into brawls and gun battles.

I recalled a former LAPD colleague who was in an officer-involved shooting once, the unfortunate timing being that it happened a few days prior to his wedding. On the night before he got married, he woke up at 3:00 am to see a strange, dark figure looming over his bed. He grabbed his service revolver and ordered the person to put their hands in the air. When they didn't move, he fired twice at their midsection, turned on the lights and discovered he had just blown two holes directly into his tuxedo. Sometimes we don't realize just how jangled our nerves can be.

I nodded appreciatively at Roberto. "Thanks," I said. "I owe you."

"I owe you, too," smiled Roberto. "For closing this case. But I'm looking forward to seeing the Dodgers as well. Up close."

"Haven't forgotten that," I said, returning the smile. Box seats were a small price to pay.

I answered some more questions from the detectives, and after some wrangling and Roberto's intervention, I was allowed to leave and also allowed to keep my backup .38. Good thing, because it looked like they were going to keep my other pistol in the evidence locker for a while, until some department bureaucrat formally closed the Mike Black case. I made a mental note to go buy myself a new gun. Maybe this time I'd upgrade to a .357 Magnum. I liked the way it felt in my hand.

It had been a long day and a long week. But there was something else I needed to finish. And since I was already next door to Beverly Hills, I decided to swing by and pay Anna Faust a visit. Maybe I could wrap up one other thing today, too.

Anna lived in the area some people joke of as the poor section of Beverly Hills. This was south of Wilshire Boulevard, an older neighborhood filled with relatively nice homes and apartment buildings. Anna lived on Linden Drive, between Wilshire and Olympic. It was close enough to the Century Plaza Towers that I could have practically walked there.

The yard in front of the adobe-style house was nicely landscaped, with a clump of vivid red bougainvillea hanging from a white latticed fence surrounding the property. This served to shield the house from being viewed from the street, in addition to adding some charm and grace. I opened a wrought-iron gate and walked up a small flagstone path to the front door and rang the bell. A minute later, Anna opened the door.

"Mr. Burnside. This is a surprise."

"I hope I'm not disturbing you. And I apologize for not calling first. Occupational hazard."

She frowned, but invited me in. Her home was tastefully decorated, and the furniture looked fairly new. In my neighborhood in Mar Vista, a home like this would be worth a fraction of the price it could fetch in Beverly Hills. Location was everything in real estate.

"Is anyone else home?" I asked.

Anna Faust frowned again. I smiled and told her not to be alarmed. I just needed to ask her some questions.

"What is this about?" she asked.

"Laputa," I said. "It's really about Jack Beale. I think you probably know why I'm here."

She took in a long, deep breath and then let it out slowly. She sighed in a way that signaled she was someone who was carefully protecting a long-held secret. We sat down on a sofa.

"What do you know about it?" she asked softly.

"I know you spoke with the authorities about Jack. And I know you were laid off from Laputa shortly afterward," I said and eyed her carefully. "And I know Jack Beale is still alive."

"Interesting," she said carefully, trying to keep her

cool, but her lower lip began to quiver. Everyone has a tell. "So where is he then?"

"He moved Down Under. Melbourne, Australia. A small town in the suburbs there called Mount Eliza. Supposed to be a very nice place. Very temperate, a bit like California. Doesn't snow there."

"Yes," she said, and a tear started forming in the corner of one eye. "How did you find out?"

"I learned about Wanda, Jack's girlfriend on the side. Came across one of Wanda's colleagues at a Starbucks down the street from Laputa. Never got Wanda's last name, but you know, Linked In is a very good way to find people. Not too many Wandas were former Laputa employees now living in Melbourne. I matched the photo she used on her profile page with some images on Google. And I found one with her and Jack Beale."

Anna's mouth opened. "You recognized him?"

"He had grown a beard, but it was him, all right. They were at a football match. Or whatever it is the Australians call football, they seem to have made up their own rules. I searched some more, and it turns out that Jack Beale is now calling himself Rich Caan. I thought that was a nice touch."

"My goodness," she said. "You've pieced it all together."

"Most of it anyway. You could help fill in the details."

"And then you'll tell the police?" she asked, eyes wide, a tear streaming down her cheek.

I looked at her. "I'm not a lawyer, but I'm not seeing how any crime's being committed here, by you or anyone else. As far as Beale's concerned, there's no law against moving to another country and changing your name. No law against leaving your wife either, although he might have engineered that a bit more tastefully. I imagine he had his reasons. Maybe he's happier now. Near as I can tell, Jack Beale didn't do anything illegal."

"I don't think so, either," she whispered.

"I haven't dug further on him, and I'm not sure I need to. I might not, if you can satisfy my curiosity on a few matters. And I honestly don't think you've done anything illegal. I don't think you filed a false police report. Or withheld evidence in a police investigation, because there was no real investigation. It was deemed an accident. But I would like you to answer some questions. I'm not here to hurt you. I just need to know. I've had a long, long week and it's almost over. I'd like to get some closure on this."

"All right," she said quietly.

"So you went to the City Attorney with what you saw on the boat that day. Why didn't you go to the police?"

Anna shrugged. "The police acted so busy. And they were making jokes about it, a rich guy falling into the ocean."

I nodded. "Coping mechanism. It's hard for outsiders to get."

"I suppose. So I knew Steve Reinhart from college. We went to UCLA together a long time ago. Oh, he wasn't the City Attorney when all this happened but he was high up there. I just let him know what I saw. That I witnessed a man swimming away from the boat that day. I honestly didn't see who it was. We were all really loaded."

"What happened next?"

"Well, a few days later, Eric called me in to his office to ask what happened on the boat. I told him what I saw. I thought it might have been Jack in the water."

"And then you got laid off," I said.

"Well, the company called it a layoff. You might call it something else. But I signed a severance agreement, for a package that paid me enough money to buy this house and start a business doing what I really wanted to do. As you might imagine, most Human Resource Directors can't afford to buy in Beverly Hills."

"So Eric Starr paid you for your silence. You struck a bargain with him."

"Essentially, yes," Anna admitted. "I was planning to leave Laputa anyway. I was sick of the place. The atmosphere was toxic. As an HR person, I was swimming in it. People were marching into my office every day complaining about harassment, poor management, nobody doing any work, and everything else under the sun. It was a miserable place to be, a living hell at times, and I didn't have a future there. I'm not sure anyone there does."

"Did you know Wanda?"

"Sure. And I knew about Wanda and Jack."

"So why didn't Jack just divorce Darcy and get on with his life, the way most people do?"

"Jack hated Darcy. H-a-t-e-d her. Bad marriage, never should have happened. But if he divorced, she'd get half his stake in Laputa. California law. I guess when they got married there was no pre-nup. So Jack and Eric made a deal. You need seven years before a missing person can be declared legally dead. And so Darcy is in limbo. She gets to live in a nice house and has some money. But she doesn't get Jack's equity position in the company."

"It worked out well for you," I said.

She sighed. "It did, although it wasn't quite how I planned it. I really did see someone swimming away. There was another boat nearby. I couldn't be sure it was Jack at the time, but in hindsight, of course it was. This was his way out. Eric paid him a lot of money to go away, and then Eric proceeded to plan his own exit from the company. By the time seven years pass, Eric will have looted the company and there won't be much left of Laputa. He'll be gone, and he can blame the failure on the executives who took over after he left."

"So what became of the City Attorney's investigation?"

"Mr. Burnside, I have a feeling you know how the world really works. Take a look at who Steve Reinhart's campaign contributors were in the last election. Eric bankrolled him. Donated millions, helped raise millions more. Nothing illegal about that on the surface. Businessmen always donate to politicians."

"And," I said, looking around her house, "it looks like someone else got a sizable donation, too."

Anna nodded in agreement. "When Eric called me into his office, he told me how it would play out. There would be a layoff of a few dozen employees around the company in the coming weeks. I'd be one of them, the only difference being that my severance package would be radically different. The requirement would be that I never go public with anything negative or detrimental about Laputa or any Laputa executives, past, present or future. If I did, I'd have to return the money."

I sat back. "So it all works out. Jack Beale gets to start a new life, Eric Starr gets control of the company while he strips away all of the assets, the employees have a fun environment because no one cares anymore, and you get to live your dream. Everyone's happy. Except for Darcy and the few people who actually care about their jobs. And I suppose anyone who owns stock in Laputa."

"Yes, that was the plan. You know, for Jack it was like that story of climbing the mountain, knowing there was this single, perfect rose at the top. But by the time Jack had gotten there and plucked it, he had lost his sense of smell. He couldn't appreciate it. He just had to get out, make a course correction. There are indeed some things money can't buy. It was a good plan. No one was supposed to know about all this. Then you came along."

I shrugged. "This is what I do. I was hired to find out about Eric, then piece it all together. BMB has a right to know what it's getting if it hires Eric."

"You did a good job," she said.

"And I probably messed up my son's chances of getting him into an elite preschool. I guess I've ruptured his bright future. The Ivy League might now be a pipe dream," I said, wondering how obvious my sarcasm was.

"No, nothing changes," she insisted. "The slot is open to you if you want it. There's no reason for me to recommend anything different to Applewood. It's in everyone's best interests to keep you happy."

I thought about this. "I want to be happy, certainly," I replied. "I'm just not sure this is the right path. And I'd like to be able to smell a few roses too, at some point."

*

A couple of days had passed and the weather had gotten a little cooler. With the BMB and Laputa investigations over, I gave myself a little time off as a reward for my efforts, not to mention dealing with adverse work conditions. So I treated myself to something I always liked to do. Being the President of my company afforded me that luxury. If I kept doing a good job, maybe I'd promote myself to CEO soon.

The USC football team was suited up in its practice gear, the offense wearing white jerseys, the defense wearing cardinal, and the quarterbacks wearing gold, to signify they were untouchable. There were a few dozen visitors in attendance; practices these days were largely closed to outsiders. Years ago, these practices had become a scene, with hundreds of fans and even some celebrities milling about on the sidelines. With that came the plethora of agents and their runners, business people whose goal was to ingratiate themselves with the players. That, of course, led to improprieties, sanctions, and a future of practices closed to all but University donors, the media, and select members of the Trojan family. Once in a while an agent slipped in. It didn't take me long to recognize one of them across the field. Cliff Roper was having an animated conversation on his cell phone. I put off going to say hello. I knew he'd find me soon enough.

I watched the team go through various scrimmages and workouts. The offense frequently lined up in a three wide receiver formation, one that typically meant a pass play was coming. I looked around at the secondary, those cornerbacks and safeties I had coached the past three years. There were a couple of new jersey numbers, but I recognized most of the kids. I had spent a lot of time with them. And I especially kept my eyes on number thirty, the aspiring filmmaker.

The quarterback barked out signals and took the snap from center. He dropped back to pass, but then suddenly turned and handed the ball to the running back on a draw play. The back darted through the line, but a defender from the secondary raced up, dove at his ankles and made a shoestring tackle, tripping the ball carrier enough so he stumbled and dropped to his knees. A smattering of applause came from the sidelines and Demetrius Goffney grinned as he jumped back on his feet.

A few plays later, the quarterback took the snap and dropped back to pass again. This time there was no fake. But he made the mistake of locking his eyes on a particular receiver. It was an easy tell, if a defensive back was alert. The quarterback was telegraphing the play, and a quick-thinking defender could take advantage of it. And when Demetrius jumped the route and stepped in front of the receiver to make an interception, I raised both my fists high in the air. There wasn't anyone between Demetrius and the goal line, and he outran everyone on the field to the end zone.

"Now did you teach him that trick?" came a familiar voice behind me.

I turned to see Cliff Roper smiling and nodding at me, clapping his hands in appreciation. Cliff Roper was a hugely successful sports agent, the type of character that the USC coaching staff had been trying to keep players away from for years. Somehow, he always found a way in.

"I taught him to read the quarterback's eyes," I said. "The good quarterbacks look you off. But it's a tough skill for a kid to learn. Defensive backs can capitalize on it if they see it coming."

Cliff Roper looked at me curiously. "You were a good coach. Dumb of you to give up such a lucrative gig."

I shook my head. "You say the nicest things."

"Just giving you some free advice," he said. "You always take these things personally."

"You bring out the best in me," I said dryly. "But as long as you're here, let me ask you something."

"What's that?"

"Demetrius Goffney. What are his NFL chances?"

Cliff Roper thought about this for a minute. You can practically sense the database in his mind working at pulling up his file.

"Look, the kid was a four-star coming out of high school. That meant he was good, not great. He can play, but doesn't have the athleticism to be a top pick. I figured him to run a 4.5 in the 40. But I may have to clock him again. He sprinted past everyone on that last play. Even blew by Allen Powell, the tailback. He's a legit 4.4 guy."

I looked at him. "Allen wasn't sprinting all-out. And

he wasn't using his arms properly when he was running. The arms have to be in synch with his legs. Yeah, you should clock Demetrius again. I helped him with his running mechanics. He probably picked up some speed in the past two years. People don't think it's possible for a college guy to get faster, but it is if you run the right way."

Roper peered at me. "Geez, maybe you oughta get work as an agent."

"Job doesn't seem that hard," I said. "Compared to others."

"There you go with that nasty tone again. Look, you want the topline on Demetrius? Okay. He's got a shot at being drafted, late-round pick. He might catch on, every pro team is using a nickel package these days, whether they want to or not. They have to. Offenses are passing the ball more and more. Got to have that fifth defensive back in there, otherwise the quarterback can pick you apart. These guys are essential now. And Demetrius makes plays. In the NFL, that's all that matters. People think a nickel back comes cheap, that he's just a benchwarmer, but talk about ancient history. I'll tell you something. A good nickel back is worth a lot these days. That what you wanted to hear?"

"Pretty much," I smiled.

"Glad I could be of service. I'll send you a bill. Or maybe you can just put in a good word with Demetrius on my behalf. I'm always looking to add to my stable. I'm sure you're still talking with him. Guys like you think that once you coach a player, you're his coach for life. I'll bet when the Bulldog called you after you graduated, you still snapped to attention."

"I guess that's true," I admitted. I sometimes forgot that deep down, beyond the tough and brittle facade, Cliff Roper was really smart.

"Of course it's true," he said dismissively.

"By the way, how's Honey?"

Roper peered at me again. Any mention of his beautiful daughter drew suspicion. "Honey's Honey. She's great. She's doing fantastic."

"Still with Disney Channel?"

"Nope, she's at the Parks now. Director of Marketing for Disneyland."

I let out a low whistle. "Pretty good. She's moving up fast."

"Of course she is. She's going places. And let me remind you, she's half your age and out of your league. I know you still have designs on her. Forget 'em. Stick with that smoking hot wife of yours. You'll thank me one day."

Staying faithful to my wife was something I didn't need the likes of Cliff Roper to remind me to do. I didn't recall how many times Roper had been married, but it was more than a few. I said goodbye and watched the rest of the practice from the other side of the field. After the practice, I went up to Demetrius and said hello.

"Hey-hey, Coach B! Glad you stopped by today. You see that pick-six I got?"

"I did. Great move. You made some plays."

"Just trying to improve. Get better. What brings you over here?"

"Gave myself a treat. I love watching practice. Also

wanted to see how the budding screenwriter was doing in his other career, the one away from football."

"Well, I optioned my screenplay, but the guy who bought it just got arrested for some triple murder or something. Hollywood's a weird place. I have to figure out how to get the rights back."

"Uh, yeah. You might want to try your hand at a new script. Maybe something less gruesome. Write from your experiences."

Demetrius laughed. "Are you a script consultant now?"

"No, just someone who hates seeing cops get wasted at the end of a movie."

Seventeen

The next few days were spent relaxing and catching my breath. Then I wrote my report for BMB, omitting the part about Jack Beale being alive and well in Australia, and making only discreet references to possible financial irregularities at Laputa. I sent it to Nick Roche, along with an invoice for eight days of work. A few weeks went by, and I finally received a Fed Ex package that contained a healthy check, clipped to a handwritten note from him, saying he would like to see me. It was written on a gold slip of paper with the BMB logo at the top. The name Nick Roche appeared near the bottom. Just below it were the words, *Chief Executive Officer*.

I set up an appointment for the next day. A pretty assistant, different from the one who escorted me up the past few times, led me to the top floor of the BMB Tower. And instead of bringing me to the office that Roche previously had, we walked through a series of glass doors, a uniformed security officer stationed at one of them. I nodded at the officer; he looked at me suspiciously in return.

"Burnside," Roche said, standing up from behind a large and distinguished maple desk. His office was now twice the size of his previous one, and the corner location provided views of the mountains to the north and the ocean to the west. He shook my hand and grinned a confident grin. Pointing to a black leather couch, he motioned for me to sit down. He sat next to me.

"Congratulations," I said. "I hadn't read anything about your promotion to CEO."

"There will be a press release in the next day or so. But thank you. Your report was instrumental. As was your detective work."

"So that was quite a nifty move. I thought you said the board was looking for an outsider this time."

Roche nodded. "They were at first. Too many failed CEOs that were promoted internally. But they all came out of the production end, not from the finance side. The board finally decided that if we're indeed a real business, then maybe we should have a businessman running the show."

"I wondered what my role was in all this," I mused. "I hope I played my part well."

"What you uncovered about Eric Starr was critical, obviously. And after Malcolm's arrest, there was absolutely no way the board was going to hire anyone with even the slightest hint of black marks."

"Mind if I ask you a few things?"

"Shoot," he said and smiled. "Figuratively speaking, of course."

I smiled back. "What did you know about all this when you hired me?"

"Not everything," he shrugged. "I knew Patty was making a third-person sexual harassment claim against Malcolm. And I knew Malcolm was having an affair with Kitty Strong. I knew Hector was, shall we say, indelicate, in the way he approached Malcolm with this information. An executive needs a lighter touch. It's all about how you communicate things. It's too bad Hector didn't have that skill. That might have saved his life. Malcolm wouldn't have had the need to go after him so recklessly. Running the man over? That was monstrous."

"Indeed it was. So was what happened to Jay Strong. And to Kitty."

"I know. Certainly, none of that was anticipated. I thought Jay and Kitty would have just gotten a divorce. Lord knows, Jay was no angel. They had a bad marriage. But he let pride get in the way. The decisions we make, well, they can have truly catastrophic consequences."

"You've obviously made some good ones. Here you are. You landed on top."

"For now, anyway," he said. "This job obviously has a lot of turnover. I heard a joke once. There's this new CEO, first day on the job. Walks into his office and he sees three letters on his desk. There's a note from the previous CEO saying wait a year before opening each letter. So he waits a year and opens the first. It says "Blame everything on me." After the second year, he opens the next one. It says "Reorganize and lay off a bunch of people." And after the third year he opens the last one. It says "Write three letters."

I chuckled. "Cute. Bet you're not going to tell that one around the office."

"Nope. But I'm moving a little quicker. They don't give you three years any more. I have to take some big steps. Patty Muckenthaler's out. Can't have someone on my team who's after my job. I'm also letting a number of senior people go. And I've asked the entire board of directors to submit their resignations. I'll only accept about half, there are some smart people on the board I'd like to keep. But there are a few who have outlived their usefulness. Friends of past CEOs have no place here anymore."

"Let me guess. Lucas Kanter won't be retained."

"No, he'll move on and teach or write or whatever it is he does. Everyone understands. After promoting Malcolm, and even considering Eric Starr for the CEO job, most of the board members are truly embarrassed. Shaking up the board will send a message to everyone in the company that things have changed. There's no room for screwing around here."

"So how much did you really know about Eric Starr? Before you hired me."

"I had heard the rumors of excess partying at Laputa. And also about the incident regarding his partner's wife. Jack Beale's disappearance was troubling. No one ever found out what happened to him."

"You believe the police reports that Beale drowned?"

Roche shook his head. "Too suspicious. The body was never discovered."

I started to wonder how much Nick Roche really knew about Jack Beale. And his girlfriend Wanda. And whether Roche had buried the bone and hoped I would go find it.

"Can I ask if the name Anna Faust rings a bell?" I asked.

Roche smiled broadly. "She was the HR Director here

a few years ago. Then she moved on to Laputa. She's now running her own business. We stay in touch. When Eric Starr's name was first floated as a CEO candidate, I gave her a call. She was ... helpful."

"And Steve Reinhart?" I asked innocently, knowing that Roche had donated to his political campaign. Public information was just that.

"Well now. You've added things up quite nicely. Anna couldn't tell me everything, but she pointed me in the direction of the City Attorney. I've known Steve for a while. It's good to have a politician in your corner."

"Or your pocket."

"You could say that, I suppose. I knew you were good. I thought you might have spiced up that report you wrote on Eric. Something about Jack Beale being alive and well in Australia. Something about Eric paying him off before he helped himself to a pile of cash from Laputa. But I'd say everything worked out for the best. For us, anyway."

"No need to ruin any more lives," I said, not especially liking Nick Roche's clever ability to jerry-rig the situation. Jay Strong had given his brother-in-law an apt name. Slick Nick, indeed. "And my job wasn't to publicly destroy Laputa, these things will often go the way they're supposed to go. Karma and all that."

"Quite right," he said. "Jay was spot-on when it came to you."

"I guess for the public, some things will have to remain shrouded in mystery. There's been enough human carnage from this case. Jack Beale is happy Down Under, and his wife Darcy is comfortable, albeit without getting half his money. So it goes."

Roche continued to smile. "I understand. And on a final note, it looks like Eric Starr is leaving Laputa soon."

I raised my eyebrows. "What's he doing?"

"Officially departing the corporate world. Moving to Napa Valley, starting a winery."

"Sounds like the party is moving up north," I commented wryly.

"He'll just drink himself into a stupor. Eric didn't really want to be a businessman anyway. That's what his father did and he hated his father. But he and Jack cooked up this idea for a business and it took off. Surprised both of them how much it took off. They treated the startup as a joke. In fact, you know how they came up with the name Laputa?"

"No," I peered at him.

"It's Spanish for whore."

I gave a low whistle. "My, but you know a lot about what's going on in this town."

"I know a little bit about everything. It's how I got to where I am. I keep my ear to the ground."

I waited. There was something more on the agenda. A newly crowned CEO like Nick Roche didn't spend time making idle chit chat. At least not with hired hands like me.

"So," he said. "You're probably wondering why I asked you here."

"I am."

"As you know, we have an opening for a Security Director. I think you'd make a good one. I need someone smart, someone who knows people. Someone who knows when to talk and when to be quiet. I think you have those skills."

I started to laugh. "Knowing when to be quiet is not one of my strong suits."

"Nevertheless, I like you. And I need someone who knows what he's doing. And with Hector's unfortunate demise, I need to fill this position quickly, and with someone good. You were a model officer on the LAPD for 13 years. I know, I checked. You had a bad patch at the end. But we all fall down. It's how you get up that counts. And you've landed on your feet. I'd like you to come work for me."

My first instinct was to roll on the floor laughing. The idea of Burnside, the wisecracking gumshoe being employed in a corporate environment was not something I ever, in my wildest dreams, could possibly imagine.

"Look, Mr. Roche ... "

"Call me Nick. And I know what you were earning at USC. I know, because I know what Jay was earning, and it was sizable. I'm willing to match it. And I'll make you a Vice President, reporting straight to me. It's a sweet deal."

I sat back. Suddenly, I had no desire to laugh. Three years ago, I had never dreamed I'd be making that kind of money, and then Johnny offered me the coaching job at USC. And after I stopped coaching, I never thought I'd get a high-paying opportunity like it again. The Security Director job wasn't a clean fit and I had some serious doubts. If it were just me, single and alone, I might have turned him down on the spot. But with Gail and Marcus, the calculus had changed. And I kept hearing the voice of Coach Bulldog Martin, and his astute words that as you get older, opportunities come along less and less frequently.

"I'll admit, that job is more secure than the one I have."

"Trust me on this. Being a corporate executive is far better than being a Private Investigator. With all due respect, that job isn't worth a plugged nickel."

I looked at him. "All right, Nick. I'll think about it."

*

A few weeks ago, I had conned Marcus into eating Cheerios for breakfast, in exchange for a future dinner of waffles. He reminded me of this, his keen memory a startling reminder of how kids can be absolute sponges when it comes to retaining information. I hadn't bothered to run this by Gail, and her raised eyebrows told me I should have. But, I reminded her, I did make a promise. Marcus was watching us, and a little smile started to form. I got the feeling he was processing something about how to effectively negotiate.

Roscoe's House of Chicken and Waffles is another uniquely L.A. institution. There are about a half-dozen outlets scattered around the region, and they've been in Southern California for many decades. We went to the original one on Gower, right in the heart of Hollywood. At first blush, the thought of eating fried chicken and waffles doesn't quite mesh, but the pairing works better on a plate than it does in your mind's eye. Some things are like that.

I once heard chicken and waffles referred to as America's answer to Peking Duck, and there are some similarities. Crispy, succulent meat offset by a sweet topping and wrapped in pillowy dough, made for a surprisingly good meal. Whether placed in a rice cake or in a waffle, whether doused with Hoisin sauce or maple syrup, this mixture of sugar, salt and fat was a divine combination. A dish where the sum was greater than the individual parts. Marcus had no complaints. Neither did I. And after a few bites, Gail too, had given in.

"All right," she said. "I admit this is good. Not what I expected. But good."

"Got to keep an open mind," I said as I cut up pieces of chicken and slipped them onto Marcus's plate. He used his fingers to fold them inside a piece of maple-soaked waffle and then dipped the concoction into melted butter. He didn't need instruction, his sense to do this was almost primal.

"Speaking of keeping an open mind," she said. "We need to decide on Applewood. They said they can only save his spot for so long."

"What do you think of it?" I asked.

"It comes highly recommended."

"It comes with a high price tag, as well," I reminded her.

"You had a good pay day with BMB. And this position they're offering you sounds lucrative. I don't want to push, taking that job is your choice. You're the one who has to decide if it's right for you."

"I know. And I think we might be able to swing paying for Applewood regardless. We have a lot of money saved up from my coaching years. The question is should we. I'm not so sure this is the best way to spend our cash. Whether we have a lot of it or a little. I don't know that Marcus needs to start learning Mandarin Chinese or how to design pottery. Or how critical it is to get him into a feeder school. I think that our decision needs to be more about the kid than about the school. I don't know how any school is going to mold him into a stellar human being. Applewood probably has some great kids, but my guess is they came in that way. It's how the parents raise them that counts the most."

"I agree with that," Gail said. "So it doesn't sound like you're so keen on Applewood. If we're going to do this, both of us have to be all in."

"You know, it seems as if these schools try and make you feel like inadequate parents if you don't spend an enormous fortune on your kid. Whether your kid needs it or not. Look, I'm sure it's a very good place. But I think there are other good schools, too. We should find out and go look at a few of them. Maybe we can even find some in our own neighborhood."

"Okay," she nodded. "I'm good with that."

"It's a funny thing, you know. Making these types of decisions."

"How's that?"

"You don't have to talk yourself into making the ones that feel right."

"I understand," she said.

"Are you disappointed?"

"I don't know. Maybe a little. I want the best for Marcus. The world can be a tough place."

"Sure," I agreed. "But sometimes the story has a happy ending."

The End

About The Author

David Chill was born and raised in New York City and educated in the public schools. After receiving his undergraduate degree from SUNY-Oswego, he moved to Los Angeles where he earned a Masters degree from the University of Southern California. David Chill is the author of seven novels: Post Pattern, Fade Route, Bubble Screen, Safety Valve, Corner Blitz, Nickel Package and Double Pass, all featuring Burnside, a private investigator and former LAPD officer and college football star.

Post Pattern was a finalist in the St. Martin's Press contest for New Private Eye Mystery Writers. The Burnside series has received much critical acclaim, and all of his novels have spent time on the Amazon.com best seller lists. David Chill currently lives in Los Angeles with his wife and son. If you would like to contact David Chill directly, please email him at: davidchill3214@gmail.com

If you enjoyed Nickel Package, then don't miss David Chill's seventh Burnside novel....

Double Pass

Here is a sample chapter of this terrific mystery...

DOUBLE PASS PREVIEW

They say what's past is prologue. Those seminal events that happened so long ago, the ones you think are laying dormant and buried, are really just a prelude to the future. I wasn't convinced, but I couldn't dismiss this either. There were always going to be people who would spring magically back into your life, often when you least expected it.

I was sitting in my office, talking about Noah Greenland. Noah Greenland was a marvelous high school quarterback who had precision accuracy when it came to throwing a football. The angry old man seated across from me did not have a high opinion of Noah Greenland. That was okay, since I didn't have a high opinion of the angry man. The man's name was Earl Bainbridge and he owed me four thousand dollars, although I strongly suspected I was the only one who remembered that.

Earl Bainbridge was old-money Pasadena, and old-money folks decided how much they would pay someone, prior agreements being a minor inconvenience. Earl reminded me of a portly man who recently tried to hire me to dig up dirt on a former partner. That portly man was a real estate contractor, one who typically paid just eighty percent of the agreed-upon fees to the plumbers, carpenters and electricians he hired. It was a sweet deal for him, not so much for the people who did the labor. These workers found out it was both expensive and frustrating to try to claim the rest of their money, with the episodes dragging out for years in court. Even if they won, their legal fees made the whole exercise pointless. It was easier to simply resign themselves to not getting their final twenty percent. After listening to him cackle for a while, I declined the portly man's assignment. I probably should have declined Earl's past request, too, but at the time, a near-lifetime of eight years ago, my checking account was advising me that I needed an injection of money, spurious as it turned out to be.

"I don't like that Greenland family," he declared. "They're not my kind of people."

"What does that mean?" I asked casually.

"They don't belong at St. Dismas. The Greenlands are only there because the coaches wanted Noah. The parents have money, and he's getting a full scholarship. He's sailing along on a free ride. That doesn't sit well with me. Plus, they live up in La Crescenta. They're not even from Pasadena."

"Noah's what they call a five-star quarterback," I pointed out, drawing upon a reservoir of knowledge gleaned from my most recent stint as a football coach. "Next year he'll be playing college ball somewhere, probably starting. Kids like that don't come around often.

So they get taken care of."

"He isn't that good," Earl sniffed. "Lot of hype if you ask me."

Actually, Noah Greenland was indeed that good. But it was also true that he was showered with a lot of publicity. As a high school player, some of his games were aired on TV. He was the subject of intense recruiting among college coaches. Even the *Los Angeles Times* did an article on him, how Noah had led St. Dismas, a school with little history as a football power, to a state title last season. It was a rags to riches tale that was just too good for the paper to pass up.

"And so what's your interest in him?" I asked. "And how does that bring you to my doorstep ... again?"

Earl Bainbridge licked his lips before he spoke. He was now in his mid-sixties, lean, tan, and had a strong, craggy face. He was sporting more wrinkles now, and an ugly expression exuded from his eyes. But he still had a head full of reddish brown hair, unnatural for a man of his advanced years, a feature that had obviously been afforded full professional treatment. The colorful hair did not make him look young; it just made him look strange.

"There's been fundraising issues for the team. We've raised a ton of money, and most of it's gone. No one's giving me an honest answer about where it went. But it's gone."

"You speak with the coach?" I asked.

"I think he's part of the problem."

"How about the Principal?"

"Do I look like an idiot? Of course I spoke with the

Principal. I got nowhere. They're all in cahoots."

"Maybe you should get a forensic accountant," I suggested.

Earl shook his head. "This needs to be on the hush-hush. I don't want to draw unwanted attention to the team. First game is this Friday night. It's football season, opener is against De La Salle, one of the top schools in the state. This is our coming-out party, it's going to be shown live on Fox Sports. Can't get the team distracted by any kind of public scrutiny."

I considered this. While college football had long maintained a national presence, I was surprised at the media focus high school football was now getting, an attention that flung far beyond just the student body and college scouts. My perception might change if our son Marcus started playing football a dozen years from now. But that was a big if. My wife Gail was worried about concussions, and was probably not going to be supportive. Fortunately, a dozen years would afford us a lot of time for discussion.

"And so you want to know where the money went," I said, thinking of my own unpaid bill from Earl. "Money's important to you. I remember from when I investigated your wife way back when."

A scowl crossed Earl's face. It actually made him even more curmudgeonly. "You mean ex-wife. I divorced that snatch after you found her cheating on me. Don't worry. I made sure she didn't get much in the settlement. Just enough to live on, which is still more than she deserves."

I wasn't worried, nor was I surprised. People like Earl,

aging layabouts, who had never done any hard work in their lives, had simply inherited their oversized nest eggs and then spent a portion on attorneys who would protect it. Earl had enormous wealth, but was an enormous tightwad, too.

"You ever remarry?" I asked.

"Of course I did. I'm on my third trip to the plate" he replied.

"So you're in-between divorces."

Earl gave me an annoyed look. "You don't need to put it that way."

"All right," I said, and tried to temper my annoyance. I looked out the window. It was a hot, sunny morning, the type of morning that often foretells the end of summer in Los Angeles. It was a day that came complete with a bright blue sky, but there were also some streaky clouds off in the distance.

"So your interest here is because some of the funds in the fundraising were yours," I continued.

"More than some. A lot more than some, in fact."

"Sounds like you've acquired a generous streak," I said.

"I'll take that as a compliment."

"Well, it's possible then that I said it wrong."

"Look," he said. "I donate to causes that are worthwhile."

"And this one is worthwhile because ... "

"Because my son plays on the team. Austin's a senior. You mean you haven't heard of Austin Bainbridge? I thought you were a college football coach once."

"Once," I confirmed, although it was really not that long ago. My tenure coaching defensive backs at USC had ended this past New Year's Day, fittingly in the Rose Bowl Game in Pasadena. Ironically, the Rose Bowl itself was only a short walk from the Bainbridge Estate, located in a now-dry creek called the Arroyo Seco. That neighborhood was also close to where Jackie Robinson had grown up. Pasadena was, and in many ways continues to be, a very eclectic community. It was a bit like Santa Monica in that regard; the city was home to the very rich and the very poor, as well as some who were in-between.

It was very unlikely Austin Bainbridge would ever get to play in the Rose Bowl, but stranger things have happened. I knew a little about Austin Bainbridge because I knew about Noah Greenland. At USC, we recruited Noah hard, the same way we recruited all top prep football players in the Southland. But Austin was just another kid, good but not great. And in the world of big-time college football, good just wasn't good enough. Not anymore.

When Johnny Cleary was head coach at USC, he wanted to erect an invisible fence around the Southern California region, corralling the top football players and keeping them from committing to far-flung schools like Alabama, Michigan or Notre Dame. So we did a full-court press on every five-star recruit, pursuing them the way the hottest girl in a school might be pursued. By the time we were done, most of these players had seen every one of our coaches at their doorstep; by National Signing Day, a lot of them had come onboard. Noah committed to the Trojans over a year ago, right after the Nike Combine, where high school players get their athletic skills assessed. But when Johnny left USC this past January for a job in the NFL, Noah Greenland decommitted. He said he wanted to explore his options, of which he had many. A player like Austin Bainbridge had fewer scholarship options to fall back on.

"I'm supporting my son," he told me. "By donating to the team. But I don't like what's happening there. Never liked that school, really."

"So why did you send Austin to St. Dismas?" I asked.

"Oh, heck, I wanted him to go to Westridge, where my other kids went. But Austin said he wanted a crack at playing big-time football. Okay, sure, he's got that right. It's just that the more I look at this football program, the more problems I see. And I want the people in charge held accountable."

Any situation having to do with money going from Earl's wallet to someone else's would certainly not sit well with the man. And he was going to do something about it. But apparently he didn't recall our last encounter.

"So how do you know there's money missing?"

"Because I asked," he snarled. "And I have a contact at Crown Bank, where the school has a number of accounts. My friend down at the club, his nephew works there. Told me that a boatload of money came in and went out very quickly. Wouldn't give any details, says he could lose his job. Little turd. Coach Savich said they were going to buy all new equipment. New tackle sleds, punting machines, flex chutes, that sort of thing. Put in field turf. Get new uniforms for the kids. Helmets, too, the kind with real gold in the paint."

"Oh, yeah, the real gold kind," I repeated. USC's long-time rival, the University of Notre Dame, started this trend. It wasn't enough that their team managers spray-painted the Fighting Irish helmets the night before each game. They needed to keep pushing the envelope, so they introduced gold helmets that contained real gold flakes. The result was they more resembled Christmas ornaments than anything a tough football player from years past might want to wear. But the style caught on, and soon, many programs wanted something similar. Even high school teams.

"And now they can't buy the kind with real gold, because the money's all gone," I said.

"You catch on quick," he responded dryly.

"And now what do you want me to do about it?"

"Whaaa...? I want you to find out who did it, for crissakes!" Earl sputtered, reminding me once again I was weary of being hired by people who come equipped with an inch-long fuse coupled with a bloated sense of entitlement. "I want justice! That's why I'm here!"

"Oh, right, justice" I said, sighing to myself. "So if you suspect theft, why don't you go to the police?"

"My goodness, man! Haven't you been listening to me?!" he practically shouted. His agitated tone had become more akin to what one reserves for shouting a late-night burger order into a scratchy drive-thru speaker.

"Sadly, yes."

Earl continued to seem flustered, but continued on.

"Then you know St. Dismas is a religious school. A private school. And a private matter. Filing a police report makes it a public matter. And we can't air our dirty laundry in public. Certainly not now."

No, of course he couldn't. Or wouldn't. Earl Bainbridge wanted me to comb through the dirty laundry quietly. Discreetly. "And if I find out what happened," I asked, "just what do you plan to do about it?"

"What do you think I'll do?" he asked, practically yelling.

"I can imagine a few things," I responded sharply. "And none of them sound good. Or legal."

"Look," he said with his own sigh of exasperation. "No one's going to get hurt. We only want to find out what happened."

"We?" I asked, raising my eyebrows for emphasis. Now maybe we were getting somewhere. Let someone talk long enough and they'll start to reveal things.

"Yeah, we. The directors. I sit on the board of that school. They invited me, they like having big donors on the board. If someone was siphoning funds, they'll be fired."

It would have helped if Earl had passed on that little tidbit voluntarily. Having a board of directors presented some legitimacy. If it were merely Earl on a lone wolf mission, I might have turned him down. Might have. There was still the matter of his age-old debt.

"I can look into it," I said, leaning back in my chair and glancing up at the newly painted ceiling. It was time to play some poker with Earl. "But I won't."

"Won't?" he said incredulously. "And just why not?"

"Because the last time you hired me to do something, you didn't pay me what you owed me."

"Of course I did," he declared. "I remember writing you a check in this very office."

"I just moved into this office in February," I pointed out.

"Well, wherever you were. I know I did."

I reached into my desk and pulled out a manila folder. Opening it up slowly, I pretended to peruse the paperwork. I had already gone through it yesterday, when Earl had called to set up the appointment. Earl had been referred through an old colleague at the LAPD. My tenure as a police officer had just ended in spectacular fashion, and my struggling private investigation business needed some clients. At the time I was charging five hundred a day, and Earl had paid me for two days up front, although even getting that took some haggling. But the investigation of his young wife took a lot longer than two days.

"You had me look into your ex's infidelity. I followed her around for a good two weeks before I caught her with another man. They were having quite a good time, if I recall."

"You don't need to remind me of the details. That's uncalled for."

"I do need to remind you that you only paid me a two-day retainer. I was never compensated for the other eight days. Or did you change your address and not get the six invoices I sent you?"

Earl took a deep breath. "You never finished the job."

"I finished the job I was hired to do. I found out your wife was cheating, who she was cheating with, along with where and when. I just wasn't going to be a full-fledged peeping Tom."

"I wanted video evidence. You refused."

"That wasn't part of the deal," I said. "You hired me to find out if she was having an affair. I did and I gave you the details. I don't do that other stuff. Directing porno films is not the way I earn a living."

"I wanted a snoop. I only got part of the job, so you only got part of the fee."

I took a good look at Earl. He represented everything I disliked about my line of work. He was a client who was arrogant, demanding and unappreciative. The Bainbridge family was part of what amounted to the landed gentry in these parts. Earl's great-grandfather was one of the pioneers who helped move the West into the modern world. He was from Oklahoma, left during the drought, and brought the family out here with nothing more than a background in farming wheat. As Los Angeles grew, he saw an opportunity and opened a bakery. It did well, so he opened another and then another. Pretty soon, Bainbridge was churning out the brand of white bread that generations of Angelinos grew up eating.

The Bainbridge Bakeries had been a family business, handed down through the generations. But by the time the mantle should have been passed to Earl, his family had turned it into the Bainbridge Corporation, a publicly traded entity, and Earl was simply a very large shareholder. Earl didn't need to run the business, all he needed to do was oversee the massive wealth that had fallen into his lap. And protecting assets was one thing Earl did remarkably well. Especially from people like me.

"And that's why I'm not doing business with you," I countered, pointing to the door. "I work for a living. I need to get paid for what I do."

Earl took a deep breath. Instead of getting up and leaving, he slumped deeper in the chair. His defiance was humbled and he looked frustrated. He thought for a moment and then spoke.

"Look," he said, "I need someone like you."

"That's funny. I don't need someone like you."

"I ... I need someone with a background in football. Someone who can do an investigation properly. There aren't a lot of snoops like you out there."

"And you can stop calling me a snoop. I'm a private investigator. And I charge fifteen hundred a day now."

Earl's eyes widened when he heard the figure. My normal fee was now a thousand a day, but I sometimes lowered it if the client was not financially secure. For people like Earl, the fee was jacked up accordingly.

"All right," he said finally, his mouth tightened, as he drew a checkbook out of his pocket. "But I want you to turn that football program at St. Dismas upside down. I want to know everything about everything."

"Sure," I said. If there was one thing I was good at, it was poking at an issue until I learned more than I anticipated. Or sometimes more than I wanted to. I wondered if Earl was prepared for that.

"You'll probably want a two-day retainer," he said. "Like last time."

"No," I said.

"No?"

"What I want is a four-day retainer, because I think I'll need at least four days to do a thorough investigation. If it's less, I'll give you a refund."

"That's six thousand dollars you want me to fork over," he said, lowering his eyes. "And I'm supposed to trust you to keep your own hours?"

"Yes. That's exactly what you're supposed to do. Don't worry. Unlike you, I'm honest when it comes to money."

Earl scowled. "You have a nasty way about you."

"Sure," I said. "And it's not six thousand dollars you'll be paying me. It's ten thousand."

"Huh?" he glowered. "Just how did you get to that? You have some awfully funny math."

"It's simple," I said. Part of me was hoping Earl Bainbridge would get up and leave. The other part wanted to get paid. "You'll also need to pay me the four thousand you owed me from before. That debt gets settled before I do any more work for you. And you should feel lucky I'm not charging you interest on the debt."

Earl's anger began to turn into bewilderment. I suppose he began to conclude this was the only way he would get to hire me, and perhaps the only way he would have a uniquely talented investigator take on this case. Resigned to this, he finally acquiesced and raised his pen.

"All right. So do I make the check out to Burnside Investigations?"

"Your bank should. I'll need a cashier's check."

"Oh, come on!" he barked, starting to get irritated again. "I mean, is this really necessary?"

"In your case, yes," I said. When someone cheats you out of money, their credibility is shot. I allow people to take advantage of me once. Give a cheater a second chance, and they'll have a second opportunity to cheat you.

Earl stood up, looked as if he were about to storm out, and then stopped. Resignation crept across his wrinkled face. "I imagine there's a Wells Fargo in West L.A.? I don't normally leave Pasadena. No reason to, you know."

"There's one over on Pico. Past Westwood. You can be there and back in fifteen minutes. It's mid-morning. Traffic's light."

He turned to leave, but I had one more question.

"Say, Earl."

He turned back to look at me. "Don't tell me you have one more requirement."

"Nope. Just a question."

"What's that?"

"How much money did you personally donate to St. Dismas for this fundraising venture?"

Earl's expression turned sheepish and he looked at me for a good five seconds. I wasn't sure if he was trying to make me sorry I had asked, or simply trying to remember the amount. "A hundred thousand," he finally said. "That impress you?"

I let out a low whistle. And I started to think my fifteen hundred-a-day fee might have actually been a bit too low.

"That's quite a lot."

"Yeah," he said sourly. "I wish I had never sent Austin to that school. But he's a senior now, so it's done. I should have listened to a friend of mine at the club. He told me who St. Dismas really was, but I just laughed it off."

"All right. So who was St. Dismas?"

"He was referred to," Earl said, a nasty sneer crossing his face, "as the patron saint of thieves."

To purchase the full copy of Double Pass, please visit www.Amazon.com

Nickel Package